Brazos Fugitive

They marked Jared Clay with a lynch rope but the scar went a lot deeper than that. His life was ruined, and when the chance came for him to square things, he took it with both fists and blazing guns.

Before the final showdown, Clay has to run for his life. He is a fugitive with a 'dead-or-alive' bounty on his head and he must face killer deserts, Texas twisters, flooded rivers and treachery on all sides.

It all ends where it began: Clay stands alone, surrounded by enemies. . . .

Brazos Fugitive

Tyler Hatch

A Black Horse Western

ROBERT HALE · LONDON

© Tyler Hatch 2010
First published in Great Britain 2010

ISBN 978-0-7090-8880-6

Robert Hale Limited
Clerkenwell House
Clerkenwell Green
London EC1R 0HT

www.halebooks.com

Typeset by
Derek Doyle & Associates, Shaw Heath
Printed and bound in Great Britain by
CPI Antony Rowe, Chippenham and Eastbourne

CHAPTER 1

RED-HANDED

Six mavericks in less than a week in the same patch of brush! Jared Clay couldn't believe his luck as he heated his branding iron. It was a simple 'JC' with the curve of the 'J' acting as a kind of pothook to hang the 'C' on. He had hopes of that brand being on several hundred head by the time prove-up on his quarter-section came around.

No harm in hoping!

He had just pressed the iron into the hide and set the maverick bawling when Ryker's men appeared out of the brush. All had rifles, and they were all pointing at Jared Clay.

'Pull that iron, Clay! And pronto!'

That was Brack Longo, of course, one of Kit Ryker's troubleshooters. Clay wasn't about to play hero or give Longo an excuse to put a bullet in him so he tossed the iron away but not before it had singed his brand into the close-cropped hair. The maverick bawled, panicked, legs still tied, but the actual skin hadn't been touched by the glowing iron.

Clay stood up, sweat trickling down his sunburned, stubbled and somewhat narrow face as he raised his hands shoulder high. His calm brown eyes sought Longo, as always, forking his big black that he called Shadow, the leather cuffs he favoured, one on each wrist, gleaming with neatsfoot oil.

'No need to raise a sweat, Longo, it's a maverick.'

Longo was a squat man, heavily muscled, moon-faced but with an unmistakable brutal set to tight protruding lips. He flicked bleak grey eyes to the rider on his left. 'Go see.'

Lew Allison was an easy-going cowpoke as far as Clay knew: he had seen him around a few times, riding range, and they had waved to each other in a civil manner. But he worked for Ryker so that automatically made him an enemy. He was a tall man, an inch or more higher than Clay, and he stooped over the bucking, still bawling maverick.

'No brand, Longo, 'cept what Clay managed to singe into the hair as we rode up. Ain't quite touched the skin.'

'No brand? You sure there ain't a Circle R there?'

Allison tensed slightly, flicked his gaze briefly to Clay's sober face, and shook his head. 'Can't see it.'

Longo curled a rubbery lip, spoke to the man on his other side. 'Brandy, you got better eyes'n Lew. Go take a look.'

His tone was edgy and the look he threw Allison was not friendly. Brandy, a nondescript cowpoke, dismounted, paused to slide a blackened branding iron from a saddle-bag and walked to Clay's fire, poked the end of the iron in amongst the coals. He got down on his knees and fanned it to red heat with his greasy hat. Lew Allison frowned, glanced at Clay, who turned a bleak gaze on Longo. But he didn't say anything.

'You been robbin' Mr Ryker of all his mavericks, Clay. We've had men watchin'.'

'This would've made six – hardly noticable in a spread the size of Circle R. And mavericks are fair game for anyone, you know that as well as I do, Longo.'

'Aw, now, you got it wrong. See, lot of folk think that because Mr Ryker's got the biggest spread around, that little things don't count. But that's the way big spreads *get* big. He told me so himself, said, "Brack, chouse every goddamn maverick outta the brush. *Every single one!* One maverick bull can be the start of a sizeable herd, you get a maverick cow for him. That's all it takes. Multiply it by a few dozen, a hundred, an' you got yourself a herd that'll string from here to El Paso, nose to butt." So, just one maverick can count for heaps, Clay. An' that l'il feller's already hung better'n most men in our bunkhouse. Brandy?'

Brandy moved the now-glowing iron. 'Looks about ready, boss.'

'Test it out.'

Brandy bared his worn, ugly teeth as he placed a boot on the hip of the trussed maverick and burned a Circle R brand deep into the hide. The beast really bucked and bawled this time and Clay moved his head aside from the rise of the stinking smoke.

'Hey, Longo!' Brandy said, squinting at the maverick now. 'This'n's wearin' Mr Ryker's brand on the right hip!'

'Then it belongs to Circle R,' Longo said, grinning crookedly at Clay. 'We always brand on the right hip. You got yourself some trouble, Clay. You been caught red-handed tryin' to runnin'-iron Mr Ryker's brand. That's rustlin' in my book. Huh, fellers?'

The other riders all agreed, except Lew Allison, but Longo ignored his non-answer, stood in the stirrups, looking around. He pointed.

'How about that big post oak yonder? You oughta get a good view from up in them branches, Clay!'

Jared Clay stiffened, not believing this. 'You're gonna lynch me?'

Longo shrugged. 'That's what you do with fellers caught rustlin' red-handed. Law of the range.'

'I didn't know Ryker wanted my land so bad!'

Longo chuckled. 'Storm season hereabouts, right now, Clay. You oughta check out land proper when you figure to prove-up on it. Last big storm we had, a cliff fell down smack into Yellow Creek. Why you think you got such good water on this here quarter-section?' He leaned forward, big hands on his saddlehorn. 'Because it's rightfully Mr Ryker's water! Damn crick changed course, cut clear through your section, before Mr Ryker could get his monicker on the prove-up papers. You beat him by a whisker – and he ain't happy.'

'First come, first served.'

Longo laughed louder. 'You b'lieve that?' He shook his shaggy head. 'Man, you are even a bigger damn fool than I figured! You ain't in some piss-ant county, back of Amarillo! You're in *Ryker County*! An' that name ought to tell you somethin' – Mr Ryker's pappy opened up this land. He's gone now but Kit Ryker's got the legacy an' he aims to follow in his pappy's footsteps, expandin' Circle R to the biggest spread in Texas, mebbe even the whole damned country.'

'His old man was a lyncher, too?'

Longo lunged Shadow at Clay who was a shade slow getting out of the way. A scuffed boot skidded along his jaw and knocked him sprawling. Clay rolled through the fire, caught a kick from the still convulsing maverick and then lunged up with the hot branding iron.

Longo was leaning from the saddle with his rifle ready to club Clay. The branding iron smashed the rifle from his grip. Then the hardcase screamed as the still-hot iron plunged through his shirt, smoking, and seared his hairy chest.

He reared back and slid from the saddle. As he hit the ground, Clay kicked him in the head and Longo stretched out, moaning, semi-conscious.

Then Lew Allison kicked Clay in the back, sending him staggering. Brandy hooked him on the side of the neck, managed to get his head out of the way of the swinging branding iron. Then the other Circle R man, still mounted, reached out of the saddle with his rifle and smashed the butt against the back of Clay's head, driving him to his knees.

He collapsed in a moaning heap right alongside the still struggling maverick, surrounded by hostile Circle R riders. The cowboy who had clubbed him with the rifle, Stew Sundeen, had leathered the weapon and, now, grim-faced, began shaking out a loop in his lariat.

That year, one of the biggest twisters ever spawned roared in out of the Gulf. After virtually wiping Galveston off the map, it laid a trail of death and destruction along a meandering path that more or less followed the twists and turns of the Brazos River and demolished most of Waco.

Shingles thrummed through the air like flocks of migrating geese; roofs wrenched free, spun erratically, and were found in the tops of the few trees left standing; entire houses disappeared, leaving only the marks of their foundations on the whipped-clean earth. Animals – and a few people – were sucked up by the vortex, never to be seen again. Even a couple of root cellars were plucked clean out of the ground. The countryside for miles around was littered with shattered timber, piled and strewn about like thousands of giant broken matchsticks.

The tornado thundered on, continuing to deal out death and terror as it headed for the distant Fort Worth-Dallas area. But somewhere along the line it lost its punch, flooded a few small towns, then dwindled away into a series of weakening storms.

The stunned survivors of Waco didn't give a good goddamn what happened to the twister after it had passed, as long as the son of a bitching thing didn't return.

The devastation in the town was massive and total; it would take weeks, maybe months, to clear the debris before rebuilding could even begin.

People from miles around who had been lucky enough to miss the tornado's unpredictable path turned up to help. Ranches put round-ups and major chores on hold, sent in whole crews, tools, whatever equipment they could spare. Every able man, woman and child lent a hand to the best of their capabilities and talents. The older women kept up the hot coffee and meals, provided beds for exhausted workers.

It still wasn't enough. Progress was far too slow.

The army sent in soldiers from Fort Brazos but there was trouble brewing with the Indians who had nothing but whatever clothes they stood in: it was obvious that it was still going to take months to get the town up and running again. Most of the soldiers were recalled to army duty.

Then local sheriff, Owen Jago, came up with a suggestion: 'We got us a chaingang and a heap of men workin' on the rockpile out at the local prison at Brazosville, able-bodied an' doin' work they don't need to be doin'. Turnin' rocks into gravel and dust, stockpilin' it – for what? Mebbe to use *sometime*, if anyone can think what to do with it. Why don't we bring all that muscle in here and put it to work for us?'

There were complaints and protests right from the start, of course, but when folk paused to think a little, *all that hard muscle and sweat and energy going to waste*

11

when the damn convicts could really repay their debts to society by helping rebuild Waco. . . .

Within three days, eighty-four fit and hardened criminals were brought in to Waco in wagons and caged drays and put to work, under the supervision of vigilant and mostly brutal guards.

One of them was Jared Clay.

CHAPTER 2

DISASTER

There was a short white scar above his left eye, not quite covered by the brow: when he had fallen after he had been knocked down by Sundeen's rifle butt, he landed next to the still-trussed and frightened maverick. One of its flailing hoofs had split the skin above his eye.

But he bore another scar that would be more memorable: a ropeburn on the left side of his neck. It could be easily covered with a neckerchief, but neckerchiefs weren't allowed in Brazosville Penitentiary.

He thought he was a dead man, when they had dropped the noose over his head, tossed the free end of Sundeen's rope over a high branch of the post oak and began to haul him up. His feet dangled and kicked involuntarily, ears roaring, nostrils congested, eyes beginning to bulge, the whole world and the staring white faces of Circle R hands, led by Longo, fading rapidly as a growing redness swirled about him.

Then angry voices penetrated the red-tinged blackness that was engulfing him. A sensation of falling rapidly, the jarring grind as his boots struck earth and rammed his knees up into his chest as he sprawled. . . .

'Goddammit, Brack! What the hell're you doin'?' Even through the thunderous roaring in his head, Clay recognized the stentorian voice of Kit Ryker. He lay on his side, someone fumbling to untie the rope binding his hands behind him; the noose apparently had already been removed but he had no recollection of that happening.

'Caught him usin' a runnin'-iron on one of our mavericks we'd already branded, boss.'

'I saw that brand, Brack, raw and fresh. You're a damn fool. Owen Jago's not an idiot. He'd read the sign like a newspaper headline. You set it up just to swing Clay.'

'Thought that's what you'd want.'

'I want his land but I *don't* want to tangle with Jago. He knows all about lynching a rustler on the spot, but you don't do it in his bailiwick! Christ almighty, you were *there* the day he rode out to the ranch to spell it out for me. Besides, I can't have a lynchin' when Carrie's getting ready to marry the son of Congressman Hamilton Ball. *That's* worth a lot more to me than any piss-ant quarter-section. I gotta be a good boy, not take the law into my own hands with these damn nesters.'

'Wouldn't be the first time.'

'Shut up, Brack! If someone hadn't fired a gun and I

14

heard it, we'd be facing a murder charge by now!'

Longo's voice was suddenly bitter, no longer defensive. 'That was Allison – shot at a snake, he reckons.'

'It ran under the rocks,' Lew Allison said quietly. 'I missed it. Hell, most of you men would've done the same if you'd seen a rattler that close to where we were standin'.'

'Yeah, *if* we'd seen a snake! No one else seen it except you, Mr Quick-on-the-trigger!'

Allison didn't answer Longo's veiled accusation.

'Well, boss, what we do with Clay now? He's comin' round, starin' up.' Longo laughed briefly. 'Oooh! Look at them eyes! I can feel the shivers runnin' down my back!'

'Take note of 'em, Longo,' grated Clay with a massive effort, groggily trying to sit up.

'Damn! Now I ain't gonna sleep tonight, worryin' about Clay comin' after me!'

Sundeen chuckled but Kit Ryder, a medium-sized man with a deep, barrel chest and close-cropped black beard and sideburns which made him look quite distinguished, said, 'You can sleep easy. Jared Clay's goin' to jail – for rustling.'

A pause and then Longo swore. 'Judas! You gonna pin rustlin' on him after all! Christ, he coulda been swingin' high by now and this section'd be yours for the takin'.'

'I told you: I can't afford to run afoul of Jago. I've got to be *seen* to do the right thing, for Carrie's sake. We've got a chance to do this legal now. Throw Clay in jail and he automatically loses this quarter-section, and can never get another, after a rustling conviction.'

'You gonna file on it, then?'

'Lew here is gonna file on it. He's gonna prove-up on it, with any help he needs from Circle R, and when it's done in his name, I'll buy it back from him. You agreeable to that, Lew?'

'Hell, yeah! That's a right good deal, Mr Ryker.'

'Damn right it is!' gritted Longo, glaring at Allison. 'You damn well knew what you were doin', shootin' at that imaginary snake, din' you? Knew Kit was within hearin'.'

Allison arched his eyebrows. 'I told you—'

'Aw, shut up, Lew! You was always the odd one out in the crew.' He flicked a quick glance at the rancher, then back to Allison. 'You know which side your bread's buttered on.' Longo pulled his shirt out and looked at his scorched chest, turning to kick Clay.

'Quit that! Lew's got some brains and he uses them,' Ryker said. He moved and stood above the semi-conscious Clay who was sitting up, covered by Sundeen, rubbing his aching throat. Ryker's boot nudged him in the ribs. 'You should've taken my offer weeks ago, drifter.'

'And mebbe, just mebbe, you should've let Longo hang me.'

Ryker was startled by the threat coming so balefully from a man in such distress. For a moment blood drained from his heavy-featured face. Then he curled a lip and kicked Clay hard in the ribs, twice, and once more on a shoulder.

16

'Brack, looks to me like this damn nester is takin' things just a mite *too* casually. Hell! I'd've expected him to put up a decent sort of fight and here he is, hardly a mark on him.'

He said no more, just stood there, hands on big hips, looking down at Clay, who suddenly surged to his feet, launched himself as if from a catapult and smashed the top of his head into the middle of the rancher's face.

His move took them all by surprise, not the least Kit Ryker himself. The rancher shot backwards six feet, blood spurting from mashed nostrils and crushed lips. He stumbled and would have fallen to one knee except Lew Allison steadied him. Sundeen hit Clay in the kidneys and as the man sagged to his knees drove three more hard blows into him, before he spread out, writhing.

Longo helped steady Ryker, who was shaking his head, blinking, spitting blood and broken teeth.

'Sure you ain't changed your mind about that lynchin', boss?'

Ryker, wet, reddened eyes swivelling, shook his head savagely, wincing at the pain. '*No*! He lives – for now. But he don't have to live without pain! Get him on his feet!'

The rancher's big hands were already bloodied from his own wounds and as Sundeen and Allison held Clay's arms, Kit set his feet and his arms worked like pistons, around Clay's rib cage, up and down his chest, smashing into his face, jarring his head on his shoulders.

Clay sagged and Ryker, panting, nodded to Longo

whose eagerness was almost jumping clear out of the man.

Afterwards, Sundeen and Longo, both breathless, rubbing sore knuckles, stood over the battered and bloodied Clay, looking to Ryker now.

'Get him on his horse and we'll take him to town. Man must be a damn fool to put up a fight after bein' caught red-handed. Think he'd have enough sense to give up, instead of tryin' to tackle us all, the way he did. Right, boys?'

Judge Norwell could read between the lines, but he had been a good friend of Hiram Ryker, Kit's father, and he also knew that Ryker's sister, young Carrie, a mighty popular stage singer in San Antone, was being courted by Harrison Ball, son of Congressman Ball in Washington. So, looking to the future (*his* future) the judge sentenced Jared Clay to five years hard time on the Brazosville rockpile.

Ryker had appeared in court, head swathed in bandages, a plaster shield over his squashed nose. His voice was raspy and slurred, as he turned to the judge.

'Five years! Judge, I was lookin' for at least ten for this ranny! Lookit he done to my face! I make visits to the Meat Agencies in Chicago and Philadelphia. I meet with the top men, as you know, respected men with high reputations, high standing in society. Why, if Carrie marries young Ball I'll. . . . How you think it's gonna look me turnin' up with my face all mashed in! Because of this son of a bitch Jared Clay! I demand—'

'No you don't, Kit,' Norwell said quietly but firmly,

his eyes glittering. 'You are a sorry sight, I admit, but neither you nor anyone else on your side of my bench *demands* anything in my court.' He wanted that understood, no matter what.

Ryker swallowed, nodding jerkily. 'I . . . I apologize, Judge. Got carried away. But, this man has caused me some . . . well, I'll call it an "upset" to be polite, Judge, but I've been accepted by Chicago and Philly society because I was . . . presentable . . . now I—'

The judge held up a hand. 'My powers allow me a maximum sentence of five years in this case, Kit. I've added the "hard time" in deference to your father's memory as much as what's happened to you. Now, that's all I can do.' He slammed down the gavel and Ryker knew that was it.

That had been five months and eleven days ago. Now here he was, knee-deep in the ruins of Waco, chained at night in a special barbed-wire enclosure under armed guard, but working hands-free and without leg shackles during the day.

It must be only a matter of time before some opportunity for escape presented itself. . . .

He had to believe that.

He was finished here in Brazos County, anyway. Ryker had seen to that. He had been right: if a man had a conviction against him, he could never again be eligible for Government Prove-up Land. So his plans for a small ranch of his own, maybe built up into a bigger place in years to come, were over. He'd never be able to afford to buy land outright.

Four-and-a-half years more to serve on the rockpile did not appeal to him. He hated the confinement and had had no hesitation in volunteering for the Waco clean-up. He had kept a low profile behind Brazosville's stockade, doing no more than was required, but staying within the rules. He was considered a low risk as a trouble-maker or potential escapee: they figured he had learned his lesson. Not that anyone had ever successfully escaped from Brazosville. Those who had attempted it were invariably dragged back to whiplash punishment and harsher conditions than they had ever thought possible.

But *this* chance had landed in his lap now and he didn't aim to pass it up. Patience was what was necessary and he had plenty of that he could call upon when needed.

There was only one other prisoner he was in any way friendly with. It was mighty hard to make any 'friends' in Brazosville: no talking was allowed – on the rockpile, in the dormitory, not even at the long, stained and warped plank tables where pigswill masquerading as jail food was served. Mostly, the guards turned a deaf ear and a blind eye at such times, allowed a few words to be passed. At night, lying chained to the long, narrow and *hard* raised plank platform that was the communal bed, there was always whispering. Dewey Tilton somehow always found a way to be alongside Jared Clay. He was a young-looking convict but was in his early thirties according to him. He was smart enough without the rat-cunning displayed by some other prisoners, and he had attached himself to Clay simply because he considered him a man who had died and come back.

'*What did you see? Was there a gate or a wall you had to pass through? Did you see that bright light down a tunnel like they say?*'

Clay had wearily explained he hadn't even lost full consciousness and so had never left the land of the living. But Dewey was almost obsessively interested in finding out about the afterlife.

'You so keen to see what it's like, one of the guards'll accommodate you,' Clay had said in exasperation one time.

But Dewey's young face with its sparse stubble had gone pale. '*No*! I can't deliberately get myself killed, an' I sure can't go without knowin' *somethin'* about what to expect!'

'For God's sake – why?'

It was two weeks before Dewey Tilton gave his answer. He had been betrothed to a girl he described as an 'angel'. They were very much in love and, with so much happiness swelling his breast, Dewey had said he hoped he would be first to die.

'Oh, Dewey, don't talk like that!'

'No, darlin', I mean it. I . . . I couldn't bear to live without you.'

His words had brought tears to her clear blue eyes and eventually she had told him: 'If I die before you, Dewey, I'll wait for you. I don't know what it's like – out there – but I'll be waiting. I promise.'

A week later she was killed in a stagecoach crash because of a drunken driver. Using a bottle to help see him through his terrible grief, Dewey had tracked down the disgraced stage driver and killed him in a shoot-out. Luckily, his judge had been a compassionate man, and took into account the young man's overwhelming grief and had sentenced him to twenty years' hard time instead of the gallows he longed for.

He was one of the prisoners chosen to help with the Waco disaster and, of course, stayed close to Clay.

During the second week, storms returned, fortunately not tornados or of hurriance strength, but there was lots of torrential rain and high winds. The combination served to make the clean-up harder: in fact, much of the work already done was destroyed by the rain. It came down as if the heavens had opened the flood gates and rivers of mud washed down out of the hills, clogged the streets, piled up against already precariously propped up walls awaiting strengthening, tumbled and buried houses.

The men were put to work just the same, especially the prisoners, who were considered to be more expendable than civilian volunteers, although they did just as good, if not better, a job as some of the others: and sometimes were heroic. Clay was actually buried in liquid mud while helping rescue a family from a crumpled house. He had held a small girl child inches above the surge as they were both washed away, eventually coming to rest on a sloping bank. He threw the screaming child clear and was half-dead, choking, when Dewey and others pulled him from the mire.

Wetherall was a hated guard and one stormy day he was in a fouler mood than usual. He had planned to spend the time in a warm, dry bed with one of the saloon women, but had been ordered to guard a small group of prisoners working at repairing the foundations of a wall that had been part of a general store. Rumour claimed there was a cellar below ground level, stuffed with cases of whiskey and wine.

Jared Clay and Dewey Tilton were both members of the five-man gang working at shoring up the wall, under Wetherall's vicious eye. Taking out his bad mood on the prisoners, he used his rifle butt and boots at the least excuse, even if there was no excuse. The rain hammered down and there wasn't enough overhang of the wall to form a lee where a pipe or cigarette could be smoked.

The prisoners worked at their chores, one eye on Wetherall. Dewey and Clay were ramming already broken and squared-off rocks down around the base to add strength to the failing foundations. The other three prisoners had similar jobs along the length of the wall, but two of them were looking for a way into the rumoured whiskey cellar, and their digging undermined the remaining foundations.

There was a sucking sound, bubbles of bursting mud, the muted crack of sodden timbers. One of the culprits threw himself clear, yelling a gargling warning.

Wetherall saw only the mouth working and raced in with teeth bared and raised rifle butt. Then he stopped, eyes widening, as there came a loud splintering sound and the wall fell towards him. His scream was drowned by the thundering collapse, mud and water spraying, loosened adobe bricks tumbling down, bracing timbers snapping, beams falling.

Clay, kicking a length of heavy timber off his legs, lifted his face out of the mud, spitting, clawing more from his eyes, trying to see what had happened. He coughed and hawked, fighting to get on his feet. The pounding rain kept driving him back. Dewey was a few feet away, on hands and knees, head hanging, vomiting mud.

To the left, the wall sagged like a twisted ribbon, and from the tangle of adobe bricks and splintered beams, Wetherall's uniformed arm protruded, the bloody hand almost severed. Just below, rain washed a layer of mud away, and he saw the guard's face, or what was left of it after a splintered beam end had smashed into the man's head.

There had been a cellar after all: now a pit with sagging sides, several feet wide. Arms, legs, a bloody head, a pair of buttocks protruded, all unmoving.

Dewey crawled to Clay who was getting to his feet now. 'We . . . we the only ones . . . made it.'

A quick look around showed no one in sight: all were sheltering from the storm. Likely, no one had even heard, let alone seen, the wall collapse.

Clay turned to the drenched, sodden Dewey.

'What the hell're we hanging around for?'

CHAPTER 3

FUGITIVES

They were groping and stumbling their way past the remains of a draper's shop, sodden material making splashes of colour against the mud, when two guards stepped out. They were mostly dry and Clay knew that they must have been sheltering under the remains of the collapsed roof, which made a kind of small triangular overhang in one corner.

The rain, still hissing down, distorted the first man's words as he levelled his rifle, but Clay made them out well enough.

'Where the hell you two think you're goin'? An' where's Wetherall?'

Clay and Dewey Tilton were streaked with mud, clothes in rags, and they swiftly put on hang-dog looks, Clay speaking.

'Ah! Wall collapsed. . . we lucky . . . tryin' to find help. . . .'

'Sure you were!' The second guard came up now, squinting into the rain. He brought his gun up, levering a shell into the breech.

'Gospel!' croaked Dewey lifting his hands shoulder high and both guards glanced at the movement.

Jared Clay slammed into the nearest guard, locking his hands together and smashing them down on the man's rifle. It was torn from his hands, exploding, and the bullet took the guard in the foot. He howled and danced and lurched into his companion who tried to swing his gun onto Dewey. Tilton grabbed the barrel, his hand slippery with mud so that he couldn't get a good grip. The guard tore the barrel through the muddy fingers. Dewey yelped as the foresight ripped his palm.

The yell startled the guard and Clay closed, fists hammering the man about the head. The guard staggered, trying to bring the rifle up but Dewey recovered, finally wrenched the weapon from the man's hands. Clay grabbed the guard's ears and smashed his head into a sagging support post.

He snatched the first man's rifle and motioned for the gasping Dewey to follow him. Armed now, they felt more secure, but there was a lot of the wrecked town to cover yet before they were clear.

Clay made for the river, a muddy, raging current, carrying broken trees, dead cattle, wild life and human, as well as remains of houses and cabins from upstream. Dewey panted alongside. 'We can't cross that!'

'Which is why they won't figure we'd go anywhere near it,' breathed Clay.

Dewey kept up but said worriedly, voice shaking. 'I . . . I can't swim!'

'No one could swim in that current. Just keep to the bank and follow the water course. Our footprints'll be washed away in all this slop.'

They could only hope the thundering rain had drowned the rifle shot and also kept most of the guards under cover.

They had a chance now of clearing town with all their tracks washed away by the heavy rain.

A chance for freedom . . . and they made the most of it.

By mid afternoon they were exhausted. The mud was deeper and more gluey close to the river, but it was the best place to lose their tracks. The rain had eased, though it was still falling, and the roar of the river had not diminished; if anything, it seemed louder to Clay. The wreckage of the town lay far behind them now.

Dewey Tilton wasn't as fit as Clay and slowed them down. They had rested under two large crossed trees that had fallen and jammed that way in the high winds of the twister. After a time, Clay clambered up the tree at the lowest angle and, cupping his hands around his eyes to keep out the rain, looked back over the ground they had covered.

He thought he saw a couple of horsemen, well back, riding slowly past a tangle of trees and brush. They could have been searching – most likely were – but he couldn't see them well enough to be sure.

He told Dewey, whose eyes widened in alarm. 'Too far back to worry us right now,' Clay assured him. 'But the river bend's not far ahead. There's a ford there. It might still be passable.'

'I told you, I can't swim!'

It was obvious by Dewey's tone that the river truly terrified him.

'We'd be better off if we could get to the far side, Dewey. We might be able to wade across at the ford.'

'What about the current? It . . . it'll wash us away!'

'We'll see what it's like before we risk crossing.'

They still had the rifles, but no food, and it would be too risky to drink the river water without first boiling it and that was not possible.

They found the ford an hour later, and it was foaming and swirling, shallow, but just how shallow wasn't clear. A couple of trees had fallen and jammed across. On the downstream side, quite a distance down and on the far bank, Clay could see a bulky shape through the rain that he thought might be the collapsed remains of a house washed up.

'If we could get to that we might find some food still edible, even clothes.'

Dewey was not eager: all that foaming, swirling water terrified him. 'How we gonna cross?'

Clay tested one of the trees that had caught up, a stub of one branch jammed in gravel only a foot under the water covering the ford. It rocked slightly. He dragged down a breath, plunged his head under, scrabbled with both hands – Dewey holding his rifle –

and felt the gravel coming away easily. Surfacing, gasping, he told Dewey he thought he could free the tree branch and the trunk would float away.

'Hang onto it and it'll wash us down towards that house.'

The thought didn't please Dewey but he merely nodded, said nothing. His face was pale with apprehension.

Clay's fingertips were raw and tender before he had enough gravel cleared from the stub of the broken branch. He grabbed another branch above water, rocked the tree trunk back and forth, yelling for Dewey to lend a hand. Within minutes of Dewey helping, the tree started to move. He sucked down a deep breath and Clay saw the fear in his eyes.

'Look!' he shouted suddenly pointing downstream and Dewey, in full alarm, twisted quickly.

Clay hit him on the back of the neck with his rifle butt. Dewey grunted and sagged across the tree. Clay's boots scrabbled in the gravel as he strained and heaved, and then the tree cleared the ford and, rocking wildly, so that he had to grab Dewey's unconscious form to keep him from rolling off, Clay leapt on, straddling it. He lost one of the rifles, swore, but rammed the other through his belt at the back.

He had nothing to guide the tree: it was at the mercy of the currents, spun first towards the bank they had started out from, then into midstream again, slanted with a series of wild rockings, and then caught an eddy that bore them towards the far bank. Dewey's face was in the water and Clay had to stretch and strain to reach him. He twisted fingers in the man's slippery hair, pulled his face up, and then the log suddenly rolled and spilled them into the current.

The river snatched at them, rolling, twisting, bouncing, submerging them, all within seconds. Spluttering, his legs kicking in water deeper than he expected, Clay tried to hold Dewey. His hand slipped off from the man's hair and he snatched at his clothes. The shirt tore away, leaving a piece of rotten grey cloth in his numbing fingers. He lunged after the body as the current tore it away. He missed.

Dewey started to come round, his white face breaking surface, red mouth open, either in a primal scream or in an effort to suck in air. His eyes locked briefly with Clay's and then the river took hold, spun him out into midstream where the current was fast and swift, making its own waves. The man's arms thrashed uselessly and Clay was sure he heard him screaming as he tried to swim after him.

It was no use. Dewey was carried away by the current, no longer struggling.

Clay stopped swimming and immediately the current took hold and swirled him out into the river. He wasn't, for a few raw moments of guilt, even thinking of his own survival. But by now there was no sign of Dewey Tilton and an eddy hurled him in towards the far bank.

'*Mebbe you know the answer about the afterlife by now, Dewey. Sorry, pard, but there's nothing I can do.*'

It seemed only moments before his legs scraped the bottom and a rock slammed hard against his knee. He floundered ashore and lay there, vomiting river water,

30

fighting for breath.

After a while he rolled onto his back, licked at the rain falling into his face, opened his mouth and let it fill with the sweetest water he'd ever tasted.

And when he finally sat up, he saw the wrecked house where it had smashed ashore in a small bay, caught up in a jam of tree trunks, barely fifty yards away.

He began to crawl towards it.

Janet Horton considered she had done all that could be reasonably expected of her and decided it was time to return to her J Bar H spread.

It was three days since the rain had stopped and the Brazos River had fallen several feet. Bodies had been strewn for miles along the eroded banks and on new sand banks formed by the floods. Animal carcases were already bloating and tainting the air. The Army and the prisoners brought in from Brazosville were still helping the citizens of Waco and she decided to leave the two ranch hands she had brought with her for another week, while she headed home.

She had felt obligated to contribute something towards helping Waco recover from the disaster: her ranch had been fortunate and spared the wrath and destruction of the twister. The tornado had cut a high-kicking dance across the countryside, but left the J Bar H virtually untouched while her neighbours either side lost herds and most of their buildings. She had said a prayer of thanks, aloud.

After helping the surviving neighbours, she had taken two of her ranch hands, loaded her big wagon with tools and grain and jars of preserves, and headed into Waco. It was a long drive and she had spent four days doing whatever she could to help get the shattered town and its citizens functioning again. There had been all kinds of apprehension about bringing in convicts but mostly the townsfolk were grateful: they did the jobs asked of them and did them well. It was said a few had tried to escape, two had been more or less successful, but the body of one had been found several miles downstream and it was generally accepted that his companion had also run afoul of the raging flood: finding his body was only a matter of time.

Now she felt the need to return to the ranch and assess what damage, if any, had been caused by the torrential rains which had started after she had left for Waco. The muddy trail was not easy to drive her big Conestoga wagon through but she was used to hardship forced upon her by nature, had grown up on the edge of the Llano before moving down here south of Waco after her father had found a bargain in well-watered land which became the J Bar H.

Although it was two years since he had died in a cattle stampede, she still felt sad that he hadn't lived long enough to see that J Bar H was a success – only a medium-sized spread, perhaps, but on fine pastures that raised fine cattle she always found a ready market for.

Driving the big wagon through the mud, having to stop constantly and clear the wheel spokes of tight-packed sod, made her tired and she stopped before sundown on the second night out of Waco. There was a glade of trees that the tornado had missed, and a waterhole. She was not afraid to camp out alone, but always followed her father's recommendation of sleeping with both rifle and six-gun with her in her bedroll which she spread beneath the wagon. She liked sleeping outdoors and, anyway, the wagon interior smelled of damp and some spilled grain that had turned sour.

She was a healthy, good-bodied, twenty-six-year-old and slept well. Recuperated, she rose before sundown, made breakfast, rolled up her bedroll and tossed it into the back.

The sun was just rising by the time she had hitched up the team and started the creaky old wagon along the trail to Marlin Falls.

Twice she heard the slight noise in the back but put it down to just some of the gear shifting: it had been tossed in casually and she hadn't bothered to pack it in any secure way. There was nothing important amongst it, nothing that could break.

But the third time she heard the sound – this time with a definite *grunt* – she hauled rein and grabbed her Winchester from the spring clip holding it to the side of the wagon seat. She felt her skin prickle, wondering what kind of animal had crawled into the back of the wagon while she slept underneath. She was surprised when she threw back the canvas flap and found a bleary-eyed man sitting up groggily amongst the old blankets and tarps and other gear she had used while in Waco: he must have been half-smothered under all that.

He blinked at her and thrust his arms high as she cocked the hammer of the rifle and raised it, sighting down the barrel.

'Hey! Take it easy! I . . . I was just hitching a ride, meant to drop off earlier but guess I was too blamed tuckered and fell asleep.'

'You find enough energy to climb on down out here where I can see you, mister. And if you think I can't, or won't, use this rifle if I have to, you're in for one helluva surprise.'

'I'm coming, I'm coming,' Jared Clay said hurriedly. 'Just don't get an itchy trigger finger.'

He clambered awkwardly over the high, slanted tailgate and she noticed the battered rifle near where he had been sleeping.

'Leave it,' she told him as he glanced towards it. She squinted at him, with his battered and bruised face, ragged, shortish haircut, ill-fitting clothes. 'I've seen you before somewhere.'

He said nothing, watching her finger on the Winchester's trigger, keeping his hands raised.

'You a survivor of the twister?'

He nodded. 'House, or what was left of it, got washed down river. What I'm wearing is all I've got left.'

'And that rifle.' She moved closer, watching him closely but, at the same time, slanting a look at the weapon. 'Do I see some initals burned into the stock? *B-V P.* Now, that wouldn't stand for Brazosville Penitentiary would it?'

'Might do,' he admitted uncomfortably.

'You're not one of the guards, but with that haircut

you could be one of the prisoners!'

Still he said nothing and suddenly she frowned. 'Yes! I saw you working around Waco, but . . . before that . . . aren't you one of the settlers from the McLennan Basin?'

He stared back, frowning some himself, not sure that he recognized her, a tallish young woman with lots of brown wavy hair pulled back into a ponytail and tied carelessly with a strip of material torn from an old neckerchief. Clear dark eyes that seemed to look inside a man, a determined jaw.

'You have a name?'

He hesitated. 'Jared Clay.'

She nodded slowly. 'Yes, I've heard it. You were caught rustling some of Kit Ryker's cattle three or four months back.'

'No.' As her frown deepened and she prepared to give him an argument, he said, 'I was branding a maverick, but Ryker's ramrod, Longo, faked it up to make it look like it already carried a Circle R brand.'

'Oh, yes. I remember now. There was talk they tried to lynch you.' He turned so she could see the puckered line of scar tissue on his neck and her mouth tightened. 'You were lucky, and lucky you had Judge Norwell at the trial, or they might still have hanged you.'

'What you gonna do? Take me back?'

'What? All the way to Waco, through that damn mud?' She shook her head, a positive move: there was no uncertainty in it. She had already made up her mind. 'I know about Kit Ryker and his methods, and you aren't the first man he's driven off land he had an eye on.' After a pause, she added, 'In fact, my neighbours and I are quite worried. There's a rumour he's expanding into our territory.'

'If it's true, you've got trouble, ma'am.'

'Maybe it's Ryker who'll find the trouble.'

Clay felt hope rising within him. 'If you could give me something to eat, I'll be on my way. Be a heap better for you if they don't find me here.'

'Ye-es, I realize that. All right, I can spare some grub and a canteen.'

'That's fine, and thanks. I dunno your name.'

She told him and he allowed he had heard of J Bar H and the feisty woman who ran it. She laughed at his choice of words and it was a warm sound. 'Is that what folk call me? Well, I was my father's only child and he'd badly wanted a son, so I guess I had to stand in and he raised me rough. I don't believe his methods have done me any harm.'

'No, ma'am. Can you let me ride with you as far as the Brandin' Iron?'

She looked at him sharply. 'My trail won't take me anywhere near the Branding Iron.'

'That's OK. Just let me off in the foothills of the Running Dogs, and I can find my way.'

'You must've been living in the area long enough to know the Branding Iron is the name given to a barren strip of wasteland that deteriorates into a waterless desert they call the Devil's Skillet.'

He nodded.

'You can't attempt to cross that on foot!'

'I'm from Arizona, ma'am. I was born in a desert,

36

under a wagon just like this one, only shade for a hundred miles around. After Ma died, Pa went wandering, prospecting for gold ... without a lot of success. But he took me with him and I got to like deserts. Like green places with sweet water more, but deserts don't faze me. I cross the Skillet and they'll never find me.'

'If they're actually hunting you,' she pointed out and, at his frown, told him about the body found when the river went down and identified as an escaped prisoner. 'They believe his companion must've drowned, too.'

'Well, I guess that could've been poor old Dewey, but I ain't had a lot of luck since I came to Texas, so I figure if I cross the desert and make my way down to the Gulf coast, I can pick up a boat there, head north or south. Long time since I've seen Mexico.'

'Well, you certainly seem to get around! I'll give you what food and water I can spare, but you aren't doing this just to save me trouble, are you? I mean, I can take you well into the Running Dogs where you'll be able to find water and game.'

'I'll take my chance in the desert, ma'am, but I thank you for your offer.'

She finally lowered her rifle, let the hammer down. 'Well, I'll make you some breakfast and then we'd better move on. I think there are some spare clothes my men brought along. They won't mind if you use them, providing they'll fit.' She smiled crookedly. 'It won't be hard for them to look better on you than what you're wearing.'

That suited him and although she tried hard to make him change his mind about venturing into the desert, he was adamant.

'I'll make a new start, change my name and so on. That twister just might've done me a favour.' He gave her a crooked smile. 'Guess I'd better not say "it's an ill wind that blows nobody any good." '

She smiled faintly. 'No, because it *was* an ill wind. But I wish you luck, Jared Clay. I think you're going to need a lot of it.'

CHAPTER 4

DESERT GOLD

The first shot whined well over his head but it was still close enough to make him instinctively dive behind the nearest rocks. They weren't very high, just about covered his body when he lay prone.

The second shot sprayed grit onto the back of his neck, and that was too close. But he daren't move yet: it might have been a lucky shot, but it could be the rifleman was just ranging in.

Silence. The echoes of the gunfire had died away amongst the sun-cracked boulders and Clay frowned, fingers clawed into the dirt, body tensed like a spring ready to uncoil.

The silence dragged on. Then, just as he decided he ought to make some kind of move, the third shot crashed. It had a different sound. When a gun is pointed at you and fired, you know it. If the barrel is

39

moved to one side, up or down, you know that, too, or, at least, that the point of aim had altered.

This one sure had, if his ears weren't deceiving him, that last shot had been fired into the air! Straight up.

Now, what the hell. . . ?

Strangely, the answer came to him almost immediately: the man shooting at him was hurt. Had little or no control over his weapon. The bullet that had chewed rock dust must have been a lucky shot.

He waited.

The sun's heat beat through the shirt and old vest the girl had given him from a kind of slop chest of old clothes in the back of the big wagon. The trousers were denim, faded and work-stained but in pretty good condition. She didn't have a six-gun to give him but she gave him a carton of ammunition for the rifle he had taken off the prison guard.

Funny, he hadn't even thought of returning the recent gunfire. Some hunch had told him, deep down before it surfaced into his consciousness, that there was no real danger. Using knees and elbows, on his belly, he snaked his way along the line of sheltering rocks, hoping his backside wasn't showing, and into a clump of boulders.

Panting, he sat back against the coarse rock, the blasting sun of the Devil's Skillet squeezing sweat from him. But he knew by the parched feeling at the back of his throat there wouldn't be much more sweat: his body was losing its moisture too quickly now, wrung out, dry as a charred steak.

And the canteen was empty . . . well, maybe a

spoonful left, warm, brackish, tasting of grit. Still, it was water.

He wrenched his mind away from his raging thirst, blinked his eyes fast for a half minute, then used a corner of his neckerchief to wipe the gritty moisture from the corners. He could see a little clearer, though the quivering heat haze still wavered between him and the ridge where he figured the shooting had come from.

He was about to look away when he saw a slight movement, froze, hands tightening around the warm wood of his rifle. *Something . . . at the very edge.* It was a hand, flapping, then drawing back. Another movement, more to the right, and he glimpsed a battered hat, maybe a gleam of silver . . . hair? That was his shooter up there and the jerky movements spoke of pain: the man was hurt, all right, but didn't want company.

Well, he was going to get it: he could be in a camp set-up there, with water, food. . . .

Jared Clay eased out of his clump of boulders, crouching, his joints stiff from the long walk across the desert. He tried not to mouth-breathe, as the hot air only served to parch the membranes more that way. His rifle clattered twice and he froze, once with a cheek pressed hard against the coarse surface of a basalt rock. But he made himself stay put until he was sure he hadn't alerted the man who was still above him on that ledge.

The last bit was steep and he had to slide the Winchester barrel through his belt so as to leave both hands free. He was breathing hard through dust-clogged nostrils by the time he was able to crawl onto one end of the ledge. There was a jutting rock between him and the man who had shot at him and he stiffened as he heard a moan.

Nothing coherent, just a deep-seated moan of a man in bad pain. Clay took a chance then: he slid the carbine out from under his belt, stepped around the jutting rock as he levered a shell into the breech. But he immediately eased the pressure on the trigger.

This man was no danger to him – must have had a powerful reserve of strength to get off those few shots. But they had taken their toll – he would never manage another one.

He was old, maybe in his sixties, bone and rawhide, clothes ragged, hanging on his emaciated frame. There was a filthy rag, stiff and dark with dried blood, clamped against his left side, held in place with a single strand of frayed rope. His straggly beard was clogged with dirt and old food, his nose flattened with flaring nostrils, rheumy, mattery eyes either side, watching him. But Clay wasn't sure the old man could see anything, at least not clearly. It looked like desert blight to him and the pain of his eyes added to what must be a pretty damn serious wound in his torso wouldn't aid clear vision.

'You're a mighty tough man, old-timer, still shooting at me and banged up the way you are.'

The thin body stiffened and the Christ-like face turned towards him, eyes blinking, straining to see.

'You ain't who I thought. Who the hell are you?'

Clay saw no reason for not giving his name, adding, 'I'm trying to cross the Skillet afoot. Must've took a wrong turn. Missed Black Ridge, I guess.'

The man was silent, then, in his harsh, rattly voice, said, 'You know this country?'

'Not know, but I've been through here long ago. Mister, will you let me look at your wound? I see you've got a water keg in the shade under that strip of canvas, which is where you should be. I can wash the wound and—'

'Crawled here when I heard you, can't make it back.'

'I'll lend you a hand.'

'No!' The rasping shout stopped Clay in his tracks. 'I'm obliged, but I couldn't stand the pain.'

'Bullet wound?'

The old man nodded, a slow-motion effort, face grimacing. 'Still in there. Come from the back.'

Clay stiffened, frowning. 'The back?'

The shaggy head moved in a nod of confirmation. Clay waited but there was no more.

'Don't want to talk about it?'

'Be obliged if you'll just bury me here, deep.'

'I don't bury men alive.'

He was surprised when the oldster almost laughed, a ragged cackling sound. 'I won't be for much longer.'

'Lemme take a look. I'll go easy as I can.'

'Waste of time.'

Clay took that as a go-ahead, or at least not as a definite 'no'.

But one look at that suppurating, inflamed wound and he marvelled again at the strength of this oldster.

43

The man watched his face as he sat back on his hams.

'T-told you.'

'Who did it?'

The rheumy eyes seemed to widen slightly and there was a strange look, almost a flickering glow, just for the time it takes an eye to blink. A clawed hand reached for Clay's ragged shirt but fell short. He picked up the skeletal fingers and squeezed, the only comfort he could offer.

He brought water, taking time for a swallow himself, washed the gnarled old face but couldn't bring himself to waste good water on that awful wound. The old man nodded his gratitude, lifted a hand for him to stop.

Clay felt uneasy, the way those eyes were now boring into him. The lips were working. He turned his head to avoid the foul breath, barely heard the hoarse, dying whisper.

'Get . . . get mules . . . arr-arroyo . . . yours now. Don't let . . . the coyotes an' lizards . . . eat me.'

'Easy, old-timer! Lie back and rest a spell. I'll do what I can.'

'Mu-mules. . . .'

'OK. I'll take care of 'em. You just—'

'Y-yours . . . all yours . . . all of it.'

'Thanks, *amigo*. I can do with something to ride.'

The old head moved once, side to side, and there was a straining sound in the back of his throat, but it changed to another sound Clay recognized only too well: the death rattle. 'Get . . . get . . . get—' The words faded fast.

There were picks and shovels, rusted and scratched

tin gold pans, bundles of short, worn planks that Clay recognized as being part of a portable ore rocker, all the gear of a man prospecting for gold in the desert.

But here? In The Skillet?

Well, there had always been a legend of 'Devil's Gold' attached to this particular desert, but nobody really took it seriously. Some had looked, of course, without success. At least, no one had claimed success.

Anyway, there was no reason why he shouldn't dig a deep grave that would keep the oldster safe from coyotes and the large Gila monsters that somehow survived in this corner of hell.

He was worn out by the time he had finished, filling the grave in on top of the old man. He had wrapped the body in the square of tarp the man had used to shield his water keg from the sun. The keg had been half-full and Clay was a mite ashamed at how much he had managed to drink during his labours. He dropped his carbine with the *B-V P* brand into the grave as well: the old man's rifle was far from being new but it was in good condition, only needed a good clean and oiling. The ammunition the girl had given him was the right calibre: .44/40.

He made a crude cross from two of the short planks from the bundle for the ore rocker but he did not know the old man's name. Wrapped in a piece of chamois, he found some papers: a miner's licence, allowing claim to an area whose designation and location were indecipherable, as the old ink had faded and smudged. The same with the name on the bottom of the claim form – two names, side by side.

45

'So he had a partner. Mebbe it was the partner who had shot him.'

There was food and, munching on some jerky that had seen far better days but was still palatable, Clay had a notion that brought a crooked smile to his cracked lips.

He picked up the wooden cross, opened a jackknife he found in the bottom of a worn saddle-bag and began to carve.

Later, he located the mules that had seemed to bother the old man so much in a small arroyo. Four of them, mean-eyed, hostile, well haltered. The *alforjas* packs were still attached to the frames, stacked and half-hidden by some large rocks.

He found ore samples in one and, right at the bottom of the second, a small bulging chamois poke, the drawstring knotted.

He fumbled it undone and tipped out the contents into his hand: a dozen small nuggets of gold.

He was too exhausted to move on and spent the night in the old prospector's camp, rifle and the chamois poke with him under the blanket.

But he didn't sleep well; he kept thinking about those nuggets. Not just thinking about them but *feeling* them in the drawstring poke.

What was he supposed to do with them?

Did the old man mean him to have the gold as well as the mules? Was that what he was trying to tell Clay, because he had offered to help him?

'*Yours – all of it*,' he had said.

Clay could hear the rasping whisper now, clearly, as if

46

the old prospector was still alive and beside him.

He rose before sun-up and threw the packframes on the mules, having to fight and cuss the ornery animals. He left the one with the obvious saddle marks till last, It wasn't easy forking the cantankerous animal, sure not as comfortable as a horse, but it beat the hell out of walking through this piece of hell.

As he cleared the area, the sun touched the ridge and the lonely grave.

The light washed over the crooked cross which had somehow sagged to one side a little overnight, briefly highlighting the name he had carved on the crosspiece.

Jared Clay – 1878.

The mules made a lot of difference. He was surprised at how fast the miles slid by, even though the tough little animals seemed to move in slow motion. He had plenty of trouble, had to dismount and punch them in the ribs. Once he simply let the riding mule's reins trail and the critter ran off without hesitation.

He never did that again, took to carrying a rock in the packs and used it to anchor the reins whenever he had to stop and get the three pack mules moving again. They were not co-operative, especially one jughead with a rolling eye, and he remembered an old teamster in Arizona who once told him, 'Your critter won't move, son, don't let him get away with it, even if you have to light a fire under his belly.'

Of course he had laughed but the teamster had merely spat and, walking away, said, 'Please yourself, but it works for me.'

And Clay was desperate enough at one stage, with the edge of the desert within sight – well, almost: the heat haze prevented him seeing the actual demarcation line – to recall that oldster's advice. He had a supply of dry twigs. The old prospector had been a true desert-dweller, carried his firewood with him, knowing there was little likelihood of finding any along the way. The mule bit him on the shoulder and he swore, snapped a vesta into flame on his horny thumbnail. The dry tinder took and flared and, holding the halter, Clay was yanked off his feet by the lunging, trumpeting mule. It was one rough passage as he held on, twisting, spinning. Finally he thrust his own dragging leg between the mule's forelegs and they both went down.

Panting, stiff, sore and bruised, he swiftly knotted the linking lines together, grabbed his own mount's reins and swung onto the bony back, long legs dangling, scuffed boot toes almost dragging through the dust.

They gave him no more trouble along the trail and he even rubbed some rancid cooking grease onto the scorched belly of the stubborn mule. To show its appreciation, it bit his other shoulder.

By sundown on the third day, he saw the distant buildings of a town scattered across a small rise, a rise dotted with big green trees, and shade and cool, fresh water. Just waiting for him.

He rode in after dark and found a spare lot where he camped for the night.

He awoke to the rough prodding of a boot toe, blinked and thrust up to one elbow. A rifle barrel pushed against his chest. He had the impression of a tall man holding the weapon.

'Far enough, mister. Now you tell me what in hell you think you're doin' campin' with them ugly critters in the middle of my town! And you tell me *now*!'

As he sat up straighter, the rifle barrel's pressure easing not at all, Clay saw the early sunlight flash from the brass star pinned to the tall man's vest.

CHAPTER 5

BACK BEHIND BARS

The assayer was a thin, studious-looking man, but his rolled-up sleeves showed taut sinews and lumpy, prominent biceps. He was a man who followed his geological interests into the wilds after he closed up shop.

He poked a bony finger amongst the scattered gold nuggets on his bench top and looked up, first at the sheriff, a bulky man about Clay's height, named Cousins, and then switched his gaze to Clay.

'Where did you get these?' His voice was pleasant, but there was an edge of tension – or excitement – there, Clay thought, as he shrugged, but said nothing.

The lawman nudged him roughly in the back. 'Answer Mr West.'

Clay smiled thinly at the assayer. 'He doesn't really expect me to.'

West smiled, flicked his eyes to the lawman. 'It's all right, Lonnie, an instinctive question. Mr—'

He paused and arched his eyebrows quizzically at Jared Clay.

'Daniels, Brad Daniels.'

'So he says!' growled the sheriff.

'I understand your reluctance to tell me where you found these nuggets, Mr Daniels, but they are . . . intriguing. See?' He picked up one about as large as his thumbnail. 'Like a pebble, smooth edges, no broken pieces like this other here, which still has a little quartz attached from its original ore vein.' He separated the pebble-type nuggets from three ore samples. 'You know what I'm getting at.'

Clay wasn't sure but he knew damn well he'd better act as if he savvied, otherwise his claim to be a prospector would rear up and kick him in the teeth.

'Yeah, been rolled and tumbled by a river or creek, wore the rough edges away.'

West stared at him for a long moment, then nodded slowly. 'It would seem that way, and it probably was. But . . .' Here the excitement became clear in his voice and manner. 'These nuggets have been tumbled for many miles and, I would hazard a guess, had lain, dry, for . . .' He paused, looked from one man to the other, then said, almost breathlessly, 'For possibly several hundred years.'

Both the sheriff and Clay frowned. West's gaze stayed on Clay's face: he was the one who claimed to have been prospecting for years, so the assayer was more interested in his reaction than that of Cousins.

51

Clay sensed this and carefully composed his face. 'Comes from a real old mother lode, you're saying?'

West frowned. 'Not necessarily a "mother lode", not by any means, but certainly from some accumulation of broken-up ore, washed away, year after year tumbling along the bottom, travelling . . . well, it's not inconceivable to say the length or breadth of the continent . . . and then you found them. Are these all?'

Clay didn't reply again and once more the sheriff nudged him roughly with his rifle barrel.

'I'm not fool enough to go into details of my find, sheriff, so quit poking me.'

Cousins smiled, his lips thickish, his face tough but softening when he smiled warmly – only the smile he gave Clay was far from warm. 'You gettin' feisty, Daniels? You want to, go right ahead, feisty's meat and drink to me.'

'Gentlemen, please!' The assayer tapped one of the nuggets against his counter. 'Mr Daniels, there has been, for many years, talk of an underground river out there somewhere in the Skillet, an ancient watercourse, rather than a currently flowing one, gone underground over the aeons. If you have discovered this . . . river, for want of a more appropriate term . . . it is most interesting to me. I can give you a fair price for your gold, though you may get more at the bank. I know it's not right and proper to ask where you found your gold but in the interests of—'

'Mr West, you can save your breath.' Clay turned to the lawman. 'Sheriff, I . . . er . . . didn't give you the full story earlier.'

Cousins tensed but nodded, eyes narrowed now. 'I didn't fully believe you, so that makes us even-Steven. *But* I'm listenin' now. For the *full* story.'

Clay told him about crossing the desert, claiming his horse had busted a leg and had to be put down.

'I was slogging it when someone started shooting at me,' he continued. 'It stopped and I crept up to see who it was and found this old sourdough, dying, from a shot in the back. Never did know his name. Said he'd been bushwhacked. I tried to doctor him but he was too far gone, the wound was a few days, maybe a week, old, and infected to hell and gone. Which was where the oldster is now, I guess. Before he went, he told me where to find his mule train and said everything was mine now, 'cause I tried to help him, I guess.'

Cousins snorted. West pursed his lips silently.

'When I found the gold, I figured that was mine, too. So, I dunno where it come from, Mr West. But you seem like an honest man to me, so I'll take whatever you're offering.'

'You'll do nothin' of the such-which!' snapped Cousins and Clay stiffened as the rifle barrel jabbed his spine hard.

'I told you to quit poking me!'

Cousins jabbed harder. 'You ain't got a say in it, friend. You're my prisoner.'

'*What?*'

'You think I'm just gonna take your story as gospel? I gotta look into it and while I do, you're gonna stay right where I can find you, and that means in my cells.'

West was staying right out of this and it was hard to

tell from his face just how he was going to jump, if at all. While Cousins and Clay glared, he sorted the nuggets and said, 'I think eight hundred dollars is fair, Mr Daniels.'

'If that's his name!'

Clay said nothing as the sheriff put a query into his words. Then he turned to the assayer. 'Eight hundred's fine with me, Mr West.'

'Just hold up!' the sheriff said. 'Mr West, I have to confiscate these here nuggets pendin' my investigation. They could be stolen property.'

'They're not.' Clay spoke flatly, challengingly, but Cousin's hard face didn't alter, nor did the pressure of the rifle barrel lessen.

'We'll see!' Cousins leaned forward and spoke the words in Clay's ear, making him step back quickly. 'Mr West, you put them nuggets back into the poke and I'll keep 'em in my safe until I find out what really happened out there. No! No arguments. That's how it's gonna be.'

He spun Clay face-first against the wall, made him put his hands behind his back, then snapped on a pair of cuffs.

'Lonnie, I know you're a fair man but I'm not sure that's necessary,' West said.

'That's because you ain't the law, Mr West. I'm a man goes by pure instinct, an' it says, always – *always* – take in a prisoner in manacles. An' that's what I aim to do.' He grabbed the back of Clay's shirt and shoved him towards the door. 'Let's go, mister!'

*

The law office door opened sharply and when the man stepped inside, he brought the smell of the desert with him, and a cloud of bitter alkali dust as he started to stamp his boots.

'You hold it right there!' roared Sheriff Cousins, rising from behind his desk. One arm lifted as he pointed to the door behind the man. 'The hell you think you are? Now you back up and then you close the door on your way out and you dust yourself down, dunk yourself in the hoss trough if you have to, but when you come back in, there better not be any dust flyin' offa you. Now *move*!'

Looking startled at this reception, the newcomer backed out, closed the door and stood on the landing, slapping at his clothes with his hat. Dust rose in clouds around him. Passers-by paused to look, the women putting dainty handkerchiefs to their nostrils: some hurriedly crossed the street.

The man was average in size, beard-shagged, and he thought to comb his fingers through this several times, too, to rid it of clogging alkali, then set his hat on his head of long, sun-bleached hair and opened the law office door again.

Cousins was still standing and held up his hand while he looked the man over. He nodded and sat down.

'Now, who are you? And what d'you want?'

'Name's Hal Getty. I been prospectin' The Skillet for months, with a pard, name of Moss Tatum. We found us a little grubstake an' . . . well, he up and shot me, left me for dead.'

The man's outrage was edged with a hint of hurt and

Cousins studied him for a few moments, said, 'Out in the desert? He left you out there to die?' Getty nodded, and Cousins said, sceptically, 'After he up and shot you for no reason?'

'It weren't for no reason! We found us some gold nuggets and I guess he din' want to share 'em. He'd been lookin' for a good stake for years, long before I went pards with him. Guess it got the better of him.'

'So you argued and—'

'No! No argument! Nothin'. We was eatin', talkin' about how we was gonna spend the money when he just up and shot me. Lookit here!' He lifted his hat, pulled his greasy hair aside and Cousins saw the unmistakable half-healed groove in the scalp left by a bullet. 'It must've knocked me out. Woke up in the bottom of a crevice, shoulders an' legs jammed, one arm near broke.' He rubbed his left arm: the sleeve was torn, and bruised and cut flesh showed through the rent. 'I was stuck there two-three days, near dead when I finally crawled out.'

'And, of course, your pard had long gone.'

Getty nodded, sitting now in the straightback visitor's chair. 'I followed the tracks to Tatum's next camp and there was sign someone else'd walked in – but rode out. On Tatum's an' my mules! With the gold!'

Cousins said nothing, his unwavering stare making Getty uneasy. 'Just rode into town and seen them same mules in a corral by the livery. Roustabout told me you'd grabbed the feller who brought 'em in an' put him in jail.'

'You skipped a bit. What happened to your pard, this Tatum?'

Getty licked his dry, scaly lips. 'Well – I found a grave back of the camp. Wooden cross on it, made with some of the slats from our ore-rocker. It had a name carved on it – *Jared Clay*.'

The name brought Cousins up straight in his chair. Getty blinked, frowned, but the sheriff signed for him to continue.

'Well, like I said, grave was tolerably fresh. He'd dumped some of the tools so I dug up the body.'

'You what?'

'Well, I mean, I dunno who this "Clay" is but I figured if he was the one met Tatum, and he was now dead.'

His voice trailed off and Cousins nodded impatiently. 'All right. You recognized the body?'

'Hell, yeah! It was Tatum! He'd been shot in the back and, well he weren't pretty so I buried him again right off. I figured this "Clay" feller must've killed him, then took the mules and the gold. Reckoned he'd make for Barton Falls, here, it bein' the nearest town, so I come to see.'

'Ridin' in.'

Getty blinked, not getting it immediately. Then, 'Oh! Yeah, well, whoever took the mules, missed our hosses in another arroyo. We had two, one apiece. Tatum always hobbled 'em separately. Said if the mules got nervy and busted loose we'd at least have the mounts left, or, if 'twas other way around. . . .'

'All right, all right. I've got a man in my cells, calls himself Daniels. He's the one brought in the mules – and your gold. Which is locked up in yonder safe and stays there till I'm satisfied who it belongs to . . . and no one was killed for it.'

'Tatum was, by the sounds of it! By this Daniels. Or "Clay". Why would he carve that name on the cross?'

Cousins smiled thinly. 'There's an escaped prisoner from Brazosville, worked on the Waco twister clean-up. Him an' another feller run off. One body was found in the river an' it's likely they both drowned. But Sheriff Owen Jago up in Brazos County is a mighty careful man and just in case Clay didn't drown, he put out a Wanted dodger on him. I've got one here somewhere and it's possible this "Daniels" finished your pard and put his own name on the grave cross so's folk'd think Jared Clay was dead and buried. Wouldn't expect anyone to dig up the body.' His voice hardened. 'Nor would I.'

Getty looked uncomfortable, then shrugged. 'Well, I just wanted to make sure who was really buried there.'

'This pard – Tatum – told our friend Daniels he was bushwhacked, but got away. Wonder if he could've traded some lead with the drygulcher, wounded him, mebbe, and left him for dead, down a crevice or somewheres—'

Getty was on his feet now. 'Hey! You just hold up! That weren't how it happened! I was the one got shot and left! But I'm no drygulcher!'

'That's what I aim to find out.' Cousins stood and as he did he drew his six-gun. 'Meantime, you can rest up from your desert crossin' where it's nice an' cool – in my cell block.' He winked. 'You'll have company. You can tell each other all about them gold nuggets. But *I'll* tell *you* who they belong to after I look into things a little more. Through that door there, an' you might's well shuck that gunbelt. You ain't gonna need it.'

'You can't do this to me!'

Cousins smiled without humour, winked. 'I'se the sheriff. See my big badge? And gun?'

CHAPTER 6

BREAKOUT

Clay was never certain just what Sheriff Cousins had in mind when he roughly shoved the desert-dusted figure of Hal Getty into his cell.

There were vacant cells either side, but the lawman seemed to want these two together. As Getty stumbled and found his feet, the sheriff leaned back against the wall opposite the now-locked door and began to roll a cigarette.

'We got us either Brad Daniels or Jared Clay here . . . an' Hal Getty. Shake hands and be friends, boys.' He added this last with a crooked grin, licked his cigarette paper and twisted it around the tobacco. He reached in his shirt pocket for a vesta, and his smile widened as he watched the two prisoners eye each other warily.

Getty, thought Clay. What was it the oldster had kept saying? ' Get . . . get . . .' Yeah! He had thought he was telling him to get the mules and go. But could he have been trying to say 'Getty', naming the man who had shot him?

The man from the desert stepped around Clay warily, glanced at the sheriff. 'This the feller whose name was carved on that cross over Moss Tatum's grave?'

Cousins shrugged. 'Might be. What you say, feller?'

'Told you my name. Brad Daniels.'

'There you are, Getty. You're closest. Ask him.'

Getty was leery of this taciturn ranny who looked as if he could be mighty dangerous. He ran the tip of a tongue around his lips. 'You the one found Tatum?'

'If that was the old prospector's name.'

'What'd he tell you?'

'That someone had drygulched him, hoping to take his gold, but he'd got off a shot and nailed the sonuver.' Clay gestured to the partly healed scalp wound showing through Getty's hair, his battered hat pushed to the back of his head. 'Wound like that'd lay a man low for a spell, I guess, give the oldster a chance to get clear away.'

'You watch your mouth, you son of a bitch! I was Moss Tatum's pard for years! We was *friends*, more like brothers. He used to call me *hermano* plenty times.'

'Couple other brothers I heard about long time ago – Cain and Abel – they had a fallin' out, too, as I recollect.'

Getty's eyes narrowed. 'If you think that gold's yours, mister, you better think again! I'd say Moss was out of his head, just before dyin', didn't know what he was doin'. *I'm* his pard! That gold's rightfully mine!'

61

'You argued over it.' Cousins dropped this in and Getty snapped his head around.

'Who says we did? Moss just . . . I dunno . . . just up an' shot me! I reckon he'd been lookin' for a decent strike all his life and when he found it, well, he was gettin' on, mebbe a mite senile, an' he must've thought he'd make sure he kept it all to himself. He was a mite teched, anyway.'

Cousins snorted. 'Eight hundred bucks wouldn't set him off like that.' Clay locked gazes with Getty.

'He was in a lot of pain, a *lot*, but he seemed lucid enough to me. How about this: you two separated. Mebbe you got tired of looking and not finding anything. Then you decided to come back and join Tatum, and in the meantime he'd found those nuggets, and you didn't know *where*! When he wouldn't tell you, likely 'cause you had no hand in locating the gold, you backshot him but he winged you and got away.'

Getty said nothing, but there was some brief expression that washed over his face like an incoming tide over sand, and Clay knew he had been close to the truth.

Then Getty hurled himself forward, fists swinging. Clay wasn't ready and knuckles cracked against his jaw, his head snapping back as he staggered into the wall. The second blow caught him beside the left eye and drove his head against the stone. His knees buckled as Getty set his boots and began to work his arms like pistons.

In the passage, Cousins drew on his cigarette, watching with interest: this was just what he'd been waiting for: fight, heated words, spoken carelessly, unintentionlly giving him information.

Clay felt himself going down, shaking his head to clear his vision. He tightened his midriff muscles as hammer-hard knuckles pounded his ribs. Then he let himself topple forward and Getty instinctively stepped back. Clay followed, thrusting with his boots against the wall low down. He turned a shoulder into Getty's chest, brought it up with a hard snapping motion under the man's jaw. Getty's head went back and it threw him off balance.

Clay came in like a stampede: arms driving back and forth, fists pounding ribs, hooking into a paunchy midsection, bulling his way forward, using his entire weight as Getty tried to protect himself with forearms, driving him into a corner.

As soon as the man felt stone against two sides, Getty knew he had to get out of this corner or he was finished. He took three really hard blows that turned his legs to rubber and as he weaved, sagging, he threw his arms about Clay's hips, rammed his head hard into his middle, and with a roar carried Clay back across the cell. They hit the edge of the double bunk. A support splintered and one side of the bunk sagged.

Clay grabbed the edge of a coarse blanket and spun away, dragging it off the bunk and over Getty. The man's flailing arms tangled in the cloth and Clay yanked it down, half smothering Getty, slammed him brutally against the wall. Breath gusted and he began to fall.

Clay yanked again and as the man went down to

63

hands and knees, pulled the blanket clear and tossed it aside. Getty's face was smeared with blood and his eyes looked glazed. But he rallied once he could see properly again, wasted breath on an obscene curse, and weaved up, fists swinging.

But he wasn't set, had no balance, and therefore was an easy mark for Clay. Three straight lefts, coming in so fast they blurred, jerked Getty's head on his shoulders. He fell once more against the wall. Clay measured him with one more left and drove his right against the man's jaw, sending him stumbling. Clay took a long step after him, lined him up with a thrust of his left against the man's shoulder and, as he turned sluggishly, brought his right whistling in an uppercut that brought Getty to his toes. But only for a moment.

The whites of his eyes were showing as he began to collapse almost instantly. Gasping for breath, Clay grabbed a handful of the man's shirt, feeling some of the desert grit under his fingers, and shoved him so that he sprawled across the bottom bunk, legs hanging.

Cousins was standing at the door now, looking at Clay with a pinched gaze. 'You're tougher than you look.'

Clay said nothing, shoved the unconscious Getty aside so he could collapse onto a corner of the bunk. His hand shook as he took off his neckerchief and mopped his face, sweat and blood mingling. He stopped as Cousins stiffened, rammed his face hard against the bars, looking intently at Clay's neck – and the ropeburn scar.

'Well, I'll be dogged! You damn well are Jared Clay! That ropeburn's a dead giveaway. Owen Jago made much of it, had it printed on the dodger in big black letters!'

Clay said nothing but cursed himself for taking off the neckerchief. He knotted it back into place now and tensed as Cousins unlocked the cell door and stepped in, reaching for his Colt. 'I never shot the old man.'

'I've got me a passel here, I reckon. You, Clay, there's a reward, not much, but I ain't too proud to make a claim and I know Jago well enough that he'll pay it. He savvies the risks a lawman takes, knows we should be due any bounties that'd be paid to any citizen. Then there's Getty: I kinda like your theory about him comin' up on Tatum after he'd found that gold and Getty not knowin' where he got it. He'd be on a short fuse, mad enough to shoot his old pard as Tatum rode off with the gold. But the oldster was tougher than he thought, nailed him a nice one in the head and. . . .'

Carried away with his own thoughts, Cousins had paused while he spoke, hand still gripping his Colt's butt, the gun only drawn halfway out of leather.

Next thing he was hit by a runaway locomotive – or, later, that was what it felt like, he claimed.

But it was Jared Clay, coming off the end of that bunk like he was propelled by a cannon's powder charge. Cousins wasn't ready for anything like that, overconfident, pleased with the situation he had triggered by putting the two hardcases in the same cell. He yelled as he was carried back against the wall by Clay's impetus. The rough stone bit into his spine and he grimaced, felt the sudden steel clamp about his gun hand. The heel of Clay's other hand slammed up under his jaw, driving the back of the lawman's head into the wall.

He went down as Clay stepped back, the Colt in his own hand now. But he didn't need it. Cousins was *out*.

Getty was moaning semi-consciously on the bunk and Clay didn't waste any time. He ripped off the sheriff's gunbelt and shoved the Colt back into the holster, awkwardly buckling the cartridge belt around his waist as he hurried down the passage.

In the front office, he took a well-oiled Winchester from a rack, used a knife from a desk drawer to prise the small padlock off another cupboard with stacked boxes of ammunition inside. He took two, was turning away when he noticed several hats on wall pegs, likely those belonging to past prisoners and, for one reason or another, hadn't been collected. The third one fitted him well enough and he grabbed a denim jacket showing beneath a sagging poncho on a nail and got out of there by the rear door, after first locking the office street door.

He ran towards the small weathered shed that acted as stables for Cousins' mounts and halfway there remembered he hadn't even closed the cell door after him.

He hesitated, then picked up his pace again almost immediately. By the time he went back and locked the sheriff and Getty in, then got back here again, he could be clearing the edge of town.

All he had to do was pick himself a horse from the two in the small stables, and thereby have a charge of horse-stealing added to his other crimes, which included violent assault on a law officer, and – *but to hell with that for now!*

The important thing was to put as many miles between himself and Barton Falls as he could before Cousins came round and organized a posse.

And he knew every man in it would be armed.

It was Hal Getty who regained consciousness first. He came out of it slowly with lots of moaning and slurred curses. He sat up groggily on the edge of the bunk, holding his head in his hands. He rubbed the swollen jaw, feeling the sticky blood covering the lower half of his face.

His jaw ached and creaked when he moved it, one eye was closed. His nose felt like it was protruding out of the back of his head.

'That lousy drifter sure can punch!' he slurred gratingly.

Then he lifted his head slowly and looked around the cell with the smears of blood on the walls and floor and one end of the splintered bunk. It looked like a stallion in heat had run loose here.

He watched Cousins stir faintly. The man looked sick, face yellowish, blood running down his thick neck from under his hair. He rolled onto one side, coughed and vomited – there were threads of blood showing. Getty glanced towards the open door and started to sidle towards it, then checked, remembering the sheriff had told him Tatum's gold was locked in the safe in the front office.

He knelt beside the barely conscious sheriff and the man groped for him blearily. Getty grabbed the hand, twisted savagely, bringing a cry of pain from the lawman, the agony cutting through the fog in his brain. His eyes flew open and he stared at Getty a few moments, then said, 'Lemme go.'

Getty shook his head, twisted the wrist hard again, bringing another cry of pain from the lawman. The man from the desert placed his thumb in the centre of the back of the hand, bent the fingers until the knuckles looked as if they would pop through the skin. Cousins writhed, half-groaning, half-cussing, spittle flying.

'Where're the keys to the safe?'

He blinked up at his tormentor. 'K-keys.' More pressure and the sheriff bucked and flailed.

'*The keys to the goddamn safe!*'

Impatient now, heart hammering, trying to listen for anyone approaching, Getty wrenched the lawman's arm and something cracked at the elbow joint. Cousins yelled and slumped. Alarmed, Getty leant closer. He was still breathing, just, but had passed out again. Getty shook him, hauled him half upright by his shirtfront and batted him back and forth across the blood-streaked face. Cousins' head lolled limply.

'Tell me where the keys are, damn you! *The keys!* Where the hell d'you keep the keys!'

In his rage and fear of being caught, he slammed the lawman's head several times against the flagstones of the floor, which were already splashed with Cousins's blood. He shook him, slapped him again.

'Come on! *Come on*! *Tell me, damn yoy*!'

Then he froze.

There was a sound like thunder coming down the passage from the front office. His heart almost stopped until he realized it was someone kicking on the street door. Clay must have locked it before he left.

Thoroughly alarmed now, Getty stood, swaying, looking down at the battered, bloody sheriff.

'Christ! I've killed him!'

And here he was, all bloody and banged up, standing over a lawman's corpse in a blood-spattered cell.

The noise at the street door increased and he vaguely heard a voice calling the sheriff's name.

'Open up, Lonnie! T-bone's beatin' up again on Rosie. He's cut her this time, cut her bad. Open up!'

By now, Hal Getty knew what he was going to do.

He dropped to hands and knees, then to his belly, pulled himself along the passage floor a few feet, leaving smears of his blood. He stood up, lurched against the wall, leaving more blood, tore his shirt down to the waist and stumbled into the front office. The man outside was still hammering and kicking on the door as Getty dragged himself across, and fumbled at the lock.

Getty rolled away as the door swung open under the man's pressure. The excited man staggered inside, looking around wildly. He was a swamper from one of the saloons, clothes sweat-soaked, and his working jaw suddenly stopped as he stared at the bloody apparition before him.

'Godalmighty! Who? Jesus, what's happened here?'

69

Gasping, feigning weakness, Getty dropped into a chair, grabbing the edge fo the desk to keep from falling.

'Jared Clay. Sheriff tried to lock him up, in my cell, went plumb loco! Beat us both. Seen he was going to kick Cousins to death, tried to stop him. . . .' He paused to moan realistically. 'Man . . . I . . . I'm about done.'

'Judas! Where's Lonnie Cousins?'

'Back there in the cell. I think he's . . . dead. Clay must've vamoosed.'

The swamper was casting about, dithering, not knowing what to do. Finally he ran down the passage to the cell block, came back, panting, wide-eyed. 'Lonnie's dead, all right! I . . . I better get the doc an' . . . an' call a posse.'

Getty grinned crookedly as the man ran out, wondering if he had time to locate those safe keys.

CHAPTER 7

'RIDE THE S.O.B. DOWN!'

Doctor Bateson took one look at Sheriff Cousins's battered body and ordered two of the hangers-on who had followed him and the swamper to the law office to bring a stretcher so as to transfer the lawman to the infirmary.

Getty tensed some, sitting on the edge of the splintered bunk in the cell, having blood wiped from his face with a cloth wielded by Bateson's spinster daughter, Ella. She was a plain girl in her late twenties and had the wonderful touch of the born nurse.

'He's still alive, Doc?' Getty asked.

'Barely, enough for me to have to at least try to save him.'

'Pretty close to dyin', eh?'

Bateson frowned, his muttonchop whiskers seeming to bristle a little at Getty's quesion. He snapped, 'That remains to be seen. Now you can go on down to the infirmary with Ella. You don't need much patching up. Fact is, the way the swamper said you were crawling down the passage I expected to find you in much worse shape.'

'I feel bad enough!' Getty gritted. 'Anyways, I was . . . I din' know where I was. All I heard was someone tryin' to kick the door in and yellin' for the sheriff. I seen Cousins lyin' there and all that blood an'. . . .'

Bateson wasn't listening. He fussed some over Cousins, lifting the man's swollen eyelids, using a mirror to reflect sunlight into the pupils. He tut-tutted and sank back on his hams.

'He has concussion, at least, maybe a fractured skull, the way that left pupil is enlarged and unresponsive to direct light. The man who did this should be hanged!'

'Don't worry, Doc,' spoke up a hefty townsmen in the front of the crowd in the passage outside the cell. 'Cousins weren't a bad lawman, a mite dumb at times an' threw his weight around some, but he could go easy on a man when he wanted.' He looked around at other townsmen behind him. 'We'll form a posse and get after his killer, eh, boys?'

'You bet!'

'Murderin' bastard!'

'We'll ride the son of a bitch down!'

'And string him up to the hearest tree!'

'None of that!'

They turned at the sharp words delivered in a deep

voice as a medium-tall man in his forties thrust through. His clothes were worn but somehow looked neat on him. He had well-trimmed sideburns and a pencil moustache, bleak eyes and a square jaw. He was Durango Spence, retired sheriff of Barton Falls, but always on hand to back up Cousins, his nephew, when needed.

'I want ten men, minimum,' he said now, raking his gaze around the crowd. 'Ten *good* men, unmarried, 'cause this is going to be a rough manhunt. He'll make for the desert for sure and you know what that means.' He smiled crookedly. 'I see some of you have already lost your enthusism. That's OK. Stay behind and save me a heap of trouble of kickin' your butts out there in the alkali. Anyone who comes brings a damn good hoss and a spare if he has one. You can draw a box of shells from the law office here but if you figure you need more, then you supply it. Make sure your guns are in good condition. I reckon this killer won't want to be taken without a fight.'

There was a shuffling, a small disturbance in the crowd as only five men left to go get ready for the posse.

Spence nodded slowly. 'About what I figured,' he said addressing the doctor. 'Ask for ten, settle for five who know what to expect.' He gestured to Cousins. 'Bad, Doc?'

The medic nodded solemnly. 'He might last a day or so.'

'Do what you can. Get some kinda statement if possible.' Spence looked at Getty. 'You can tell me what happened while Ella patches you up. You don't look too bad.'

'No thanks to Jared Clay.'

'Is that who it is?' Spence's interest immediately sharpened. 'Thought he was called Daniels?'

'No. Cousins says he matches a description on a dodger sent in by Owen Jago, over to Waco.'

'Well, Owen's a careful man and usually gets it right. You got a good horse?'

Getty blinked. 'Me? I ain't ridin' with no posse.'

'You are. I'm careful, too. Want to make sure I get the right man. And he'll have time to tell his side of the story, 'cause there'll be no lynch ropes on any posse I'm headin'.'

Getty bristled. 'I already told you how it happened!'

'Sure. And we'll see if Clay's story matches up.'

'I dunno that I like what you're inferrin', mister!'

'Well, maybe I'll lose some sleep over that – but after we get back.' He turned to the remaining gawkers again. 'I can use another three, four men. Seems I forgot to mention pay'll be two dollars a day – two-fifty if we have to cross the desert – an' that we will.'

In about five minutes, Spence had his full posse.

Taking Cousin's blaze-faced roan had been a mistake. Clay realized this only after he reached the foothills where they began their long slide down into the edge of the desert. It was a fine-looking horse: its sleek, muscular lines were what had attracted him to it, rather than the somewhat dishevelled grulla that had shared the small stables behind the jail.

Now he realized the thick-chested, short-legged grulla was the *riding* horse, the one the sheriff would use to run down fugitives who took to the rough country in the hills and, inevitably, were forced to swing down into the desert and take their chances. The grulla would eat the miles with those heavy muscles, sun-up to sundown, go farther without a drink, still have enough left for a final spurt to end the chase.

Why the hell didn't he choose it! Well, the blaze-faced roan had it all over the grulla for looks and sure seemed sleek and fast, as it likely was: in a pasture, or in a Fourth-of-July race through town, or even weaving between sparse timber and brush at the edge of a forest.

But get the animal into *really* wild country and it would be out of its depth, especially with those long, slim legs. He had come across such animals before, town-bred, cared for by their proud owners, used to daily curry-combing and grooming, having all kinds of supplements added to the nosebag, given regular checks by the vet.

Such animals were the pride of their owners and were something to look at – within the confines of a picnic ground, or town and close-in surroundings.

But the roan wouldn't last half a day in the desert. And that was where Clay was headed whether he wanted to or not. The hills here were too low, not heavily wooded enough to give him the cover he needed. It would be hard to hide his tracks in such open country: and they would lead to only one place, anyway – the goddamn desert!

It was his only chance: he knew these desolate, mostly *deadly* places, knew it was going to be *tough*, but that was part of tackling a desert. No one but a damn

75

fool ever entered such a place with notions of coming across a shady tree or an oasis to keep him from dying of thirst.Anyone who tackled a desert had to *know* he was going to be up against it, and be prepared. But he'd never make it on the roan.

And, when you got right down to it, he didn't have it in him to even try. He was a man who liked horses, dogs, too, even cats, if their temperament was right: he couldn't bear to see any animal ill-treated and wouldn't stand for it. He once killed a man for blinding a horse in a fit of rage.

'So, what in hell am I gonna do with you, you red beauty?' He stood beside the sweating, somewhat agitated roan on the slope of the low range that dipped into the beginnings of the desert. The horse's nostrils kept twitching, sensing the fine grit in the air, the *smell* of disaster waiting to happen. He patted the neck, felt the slippery hide tremble lightly under his hand. The big head came around, great brown eyes rolling up at him, as it nudged his blood-stained shirt, making him step back.

'Hey, feller! If that's a hint to head on back to town, you're outta luck. Well, mebbe not. You can go on back, but me, I got no choice now.' He looked sombrely at the heat-dancing scrub that drifted away to nothing and then the glare of alkali, saltpans, and sand fine as talc blurring everything between him and the far horizon.

He had one large saddle canteen of water, almost full. There was a smelly, crumbly ball of pemmican in the bottom of one saddle-bag but no other food. On a horse like that little grulla, he could get across the desert in a day, maybe a day-and-a-half. On foot . . . say three days.

Hey, Clay! Since when you been that big an optimist? Make it five days . . . could stretch to a week . . . if the posse doesn't run you down on the first day.

Now that's being a pessimist!

Fact was, there was no way of knowing how long it would take him to cross the desert on foot, or even *if* he could cross it at all.

Another fact was, there was bound to be a posse forming, if not already on his trail.

He unsaddled the roan, removed the canteen, saddle-bags, a bedroll which Cousins had had packed and ready to go at a moment's notice, the coiled lariat, and, of course, the rifle and scabbard.

'Carrying that load, all I need to do is hang my pecker out and they'll think I'm a packmule,' he murmured.

The horse waited patiently now there was no weight on its back. Clay sorted through the gear swiftly, taking only a blanket from the bedroll, reluctantly leaving the rest.

He crammed the items he could use into the saddle-bags, and his pockets, then tossed the saddle and the remains of the bedroll into some brush. It wouldn't take a man on horseback long to find it if he rode within three or four yards of the place but it was all he could do. Covering his tracks took longer than he had figured.

Next he scouted, found a small draw where he hobbled the roan, gave it a hatful of water from the canteen and a final pat 'Hope they pick you up quick, big feller.'

Carrying the rifle, without the scabbard now, he started to make his way towards the beckoning desert.

He hoped he wasn't walking towards his grave.

Hal Getty was damned if he was going to be a part of any posse, let alone one under that tough hellion, Durango Spence.

After Ella had bandaged his cuts, rubbed arnica and salve into his bruises, he told her he had a spare shirt in his saddle-bag. He indicated the torn, bloody shirt he was wearing.

'My hoss is tethered just back of here. I can go get it and be back before Spence comes down.'

Ella looked dubious but she was a compassionate person and nodded. She had to prepare the infirmary for the arrival of Sheriff Cousins, anyway.

'Don't be long. My father will be here any minute.'

Getty was already on his way, moving stiffly, but, once the door was closed behind him, he suddenly lost his limp and, although breathing pretty hard, he found his horse whcre he had left it, climbed awkwardly into the saddle.

He rode down behind the town's vacant lots, crossed the creek well below the bridge over the tumbling cataract that gave the town its name, then headed for the brush.

He was soon out of sight, smiled despite his battered mouth as he imagined Durango Spence jumping up and down, waiting for him to return.

'Not likely, you son of a bitch! Wouldn't even let me see the nuggets in that safe after you located the keys! Well, I aim to get me some nuggets of my own! A *heap* of 'em. And Jared Clay's gonna show me where if he knows what's good for him.'

Clear of town, he headed for the hills, then, when he hit the boulderfield, swung sharply left, rode deeper into the field, threaded a meandering path into a spread of small pebbles.

Here he dismounted, kicked a few holes that could have been left by a horse's hoofs, then, afoot, led the horse to the west. He came out a few yards short of where the timber began and, still afoot, walked the mount carefully over tufted grass dry enough to still be springy but not deteriorated to the point of breaking off.

He was pleased with the result: looking back from a crouched position, the light washed over his trail and showed only faint impressions. These would gradually disappear as the afternoon wore on and the heat diminished and grass blades straightened to almost their original angles.

By then, he would be closing in on Jared Clay.

His lips tightened at the thought of the man. *Hell, why would old Mose Tatum give him that gold?*

' 'Cause he was always a sucker,' he murmured aloud. 'Someone give him a pipeful of tobacco and he'd remember it for years. Come across that man one day and he'd buy him all the booze a bar held, if he had the wherewithall. If not, he'd find some way to square the deal.'

79

It had blown up between them that gloomy afternoon after the twister tore Waco apart.

They stumbled across a family fleeing that neck of the woods in a barely servicable two-wheeled dray with a piece of tattered canvas their only shelter. A man, two snotty-nosed little girls and a mouth-breathing boy whose airways were almost closed by swollen adenoids and tonsils. Their name was McKinnon.

'Cain't risk my family here no more,' the man said, skinny, skull-headed, generally miserable, like the woman whose gaunt features were barely visible under the stovepipe sun bonnet. 'Been a bad-luck move right from the start. Lost our small herd to rustlers, but figured it must be the Lord's wish so we tried to prove-up on a quarter-section. Scrub fire took the cabin I was building, the cow bales. . . .'

And so it went on: a tale of woe to make a prison warder weep.

It had no effect on Getty. He was more worried about their stores running low and no chance of finding the gold he and Tatum had figured *must* be in that last vein. . . .

But Tatum fell for the sob story, gave the family almost all their stores and the tiny amount of gold dust they had panned from a creek almost a month ago.

'You crazy galoot!' Getty had snapped, leaping up and preparing to run at McKinnon and snatch the grub sack from his bony hands.

But Tatum had shot at him. *Shot at him*, for Chris'sakes, the bullet barely missing as it whipped past his left ear.

'You leave them folk alone! They is dirt-poor and they got kids to feed. The boy needs to see a sawbones. Now you set yourself down, Hal, or I swear I'll put a bullet in you!'

Tatum's smoking six-gun was ready-cocked and Getty glared first at his pard, then the family who huddled together nervously under the rags of the cover on their sagging dray. Getty didn't like the glint in Tatum's old eyes and sat down. The six-gun barrel moved jerkily.

'All righty, folks. You just git along your way. An' I hopes everythin' works out for you.'

'God will bless you for this, Mr Tatum,' croaked the man and Getty could hear the scrawny woman weeping up on the driving seat, the kids looking scared.

The prospectors stood there, Tatum still holding the gun on Getty, while the dray lumbered away and over the rise.

'Goddamn you, Tatum! That is the stupidest thing you ever done, an' I've seen you do some beauties!'

Tatum sniffed. 'That feller din' recognize me but I knew him. Seven years ago I busted my right arm, bone pokin' through the skin. Got to McKinnon's cabin. His wife done what she could, but said the wound was turnin' septic. McKinnon, poorly with fever, took me to a sawbones in that same ol' dray, through a rainstorm. He's the only reason I got two arms today.'

'You're crazy! I recollect you tellin' me 'bout that before, but the name was *MacKenzie*! Not McKinnon.' You give all our stuff away to strangers, you old fool!'

Tatum frowned, then shrugged. 'They was deservin' anyway. It weren't much but it'll help. Now we is ridin'

81

out *that* way.'

'The desert!'

'I got me one of my hunches. I think I can locate the underground river now. We can build a house in gold if I'm right.'

Getty snorted. 'You're plumb loco! You been dreamin' again. That river's only a legend.'

'You don't want to come, then don't. I'm goin' and I'm comin' back *rich*!'

'You ain't leavin' me out here like this!'

And Getty made a move to jump at Tatum but the old man shot him, scalp-creased him and put him out of action. When the blackness lifted he could just make out Tatum riding away, through thinning brush, making for the desert. He had left Getty his guns and some water, the old fool.

Hal Getty, face stiff with dried blood, head aching, blazing lights whirling behind his eyes, snatched up his rifle, fumbled his way into the saddle and set off after his pard. *Ex-pard, now, damn his old eyes!*

He didn't really recall reaching the rim of a ledge and seeing Tatum sitting the saddle, peacefully packing a pipe. Nor did he recall the feel of the hot wood of the rifle stock against his cheek, the kick as the butt jarred against his shoulder, or the whip-cracking sound of the shot.

He *did* recollect glimpsing Tatum falling out of the saddle, but then he was tumbling out of his own saddle, rolling out of control down the slope behind him through loose scree, unable to stop.

It took hold of him and when it spewed over the

edge of a deep narrow crevice, he went with it . . . screaming.

He was lucky he hadn't broken any limbs but he was stuck down there for a couple of days, finally made his way to the top. Of course, Tatum was gone, but there were dark stains on the ground where he had been sitting his mount, old dark stains.

Tatum must still be alive! His bullet hadn't finished the old sidewinder.

'And between that time and when I hit Barton Falls, he found himself a passel of nuggets someplace, mebbe the underground river, even! Maybe it did exist! But Clay had happened along and crazy Tatum had given *him* the gold! No doubt telling him where it came from.'

And he reckoned that was where Clay would be making for now.

All Getty had to do was find Clay's tracks and follow. *Let that damn drifter lead him to the bonanza.*

Aloud, he said, 'Hell, might's well let him do the hard work, dig out the gold and when the pile's big enough, close in and take it off the son of a bitch!

And Getty wouldn't be sharing with anyone.

CHAPTER 8

MAN AFOOT

'By God! – He's *on foot*!'

Durango Spence rose from beside the Indian tracker, Two Moons, he had hired at the last minute before setting the posse after Clay. He turned and looked out into the shimmering glare, face screwing up. He shaded his eyes with cupped hands, unconsciously flicking dust from his pencil-line moustache as he did so.

'On foot out there! By God, he must be more desperate than I thought!'

Two Moons had located the roan some time back and one of the posse men, Val Nichols, who had been complaining of belly cramps, had been sent back to town with it. Meantime, the Indian had scouted around and found where Clay had covered his tracks well, but not well enough.

84

At first, Spence hadn't believed him when the Indian had pointed out into the wasteland – a man afoot in this counttry? Surely Clay would have found somewhere to hole up after ditching the roan. Spence noted how the man had treated the horse, too: many fugitives he knew would have simply walked away and let the animal fend for itself.

But the tracks were unmistakable: the Indian had him get down on his belly with him, squirm around until the light was just right, angling enough to mark Jared Clay's path out into the white hell.

Standing now, Spence blew out his cheeks, ran a thumbnail under the thin line of moustache, as was his habit when he was thinking and didn't want to be interrupted. He turned to Two Moons.

'Find some high ground and see if you can spot him.'

The Indian, leather-and-whipcord, hook-nosed and eagle-eyed, in his fifties, stared back at the lawman with his dark eyes, shook his head once.

'Why the hell not?' Spence snapped. 'We see him, we run him down and go back to town.'

'Not that man. He know desert.'

'Far as I know he's never been here before.'

'He know *desert* . . . this one, 'nother one . . . he know what to do.'

Spence nodded slowly. 'Savvies deserts in general. OK. I got you. But we still need to see him. He could change direction.'

'He will. But we waste time looking for high ground.' The Indian slashed a gnarled, coppery hand in front of him. 'Sun in good part of sky now, past noon. Slant across our path. Tracks . . .' He searched for the word he wanted. 'Tracks high-lighted. Catch up by sundown.'

The posse men, listening, stirred a little.

'Hell, Sheriff, that'd be mighty fine! Get it all done with in one day!'

Spence gave the man who had spoken a hard look.

'And you think you'd've earned a whole two-dollars-fifty that easy? Listen, Mitch, and the rest of you, too, Two Moons is a good man, has a top reputation, and I worked with him many times before I retired. I can read between his lines, so to speak: he says Clay *knows* deserts. He means, even afoot, he won't be easy to take, and he must know by now he killed Lonnie Cousins. So he's got nothin' to lose by standing and fighting.'

'But we're nine men, Durango! *Armed* men!'

'And a man who knows the desert and has a rifle can cut that number in half with his first volley.'

The men stirred uneasily now, looking at each other worriedly. Then a bleach-haired man with jutting jaw and piercing blue eyes, Zac Curtin, said, 'Then it's worth more'n a piss-ant two-fifty a day to tackle someone like that.'

He looked around at the others, saw he had a couple of allies, while the others were thinking about his words: he knew they would agree with him. 'What say, Durango?'

'I say any man expectin' to hold me up for more money better drag his ass back to town . . . or climb on down and square off with me, here and now.'

They weren't expecting that and they knew from

Spence's days as a lawman that he wasn't simply talking to hear the sound of his own voice.

'Aw, listen, it don't have to come to *that*!' Curtin said quickly. 'I just figure it's worth more'n—'

'I've laid it on the line. What'll it be, gents?' No one answered and the sheriff smiled crookedly. 'I take that as meanin' we continue on as agreed.' A few grudging nods and then Spence surprised them again. 'But tell you what. Lonnie was my only livin' kin. I liked that boy and I want his killer bad. So what I aim to do is this: the man who gets the drop on Clay – woundin' him is OK, but I want him *alive*! The man who nabs him will get a hundred bucks of my own money.' His smile broadened as the words brought animation and grins to the others' faces.

'You got a deal, Durango!' said the bleach-haired man, making himself spokesman for the others. He tensed as he caught the bleak look Spence threw him.

'Not with you, Curtin. I don't like malcontents in my posse. You can quit now.'

'Hey! Listen, *you* offered the damn bounty!'

'An incentive. You were gonna hold me up for a pay rise: I come across or you'd threaten to quit. OK. I've made my decision. The hundred bucks is up for grabs, for all except you.'

'Now that ain't fair!'

'You ... you can't do that, Durango,' Mitch said slowly, half-heartedly.

'It's my money. I can pay it or keep it. If you fellers are thinkin' of backing Curtin, you might find I'll be hanging' on to that money.'

No one spoke up and Curtin swore, blue eyes like ice as he glared at the sheriff.

'All right! I can't outdraw you, Durango, and I ain't stupid enough to try. But I damn well won't forget this!'

'On your way, Curtin. Oh, leave your canteen. You can take a long drink and that'll get you back to town. We might need the extra water more'n you will.'

Curtin swore softly, wrenched his horse's head around and spurred away.

'I ain't leavin' you nothin', now go to hell!' he shouted angrily over his shoulder and spurred his mount back towards distant Barton Falls.

Mitch noticed a wry smile on Spence's dusty face. 'Retirement ain't mellowed you any, Durango. You're still a damn hard man!'

'Don't know any other way. Now spread out. Sooner we get moving, sooner we'll find Clay.'

'What about that other feller – Getty?' Mitch asked. 'He could be out here, too. No one seen which way he went.'

Spence's jaw jutted. 'I'll get around to him. First I want Lonnie's murderer. Getty's got somethin' to hide, but I'll catch up with him after I see Clay headed for the hangman. Now, for Chris'sakes, let's get *moving*!'

Curtin had done posse work before, once or twice when Spence had been sheriff, but also for lawmen in Colorado. One time they'd stayed out for three weeks in blizzards to run down a bunch of outlaws who earned the name of the Tri-State Killers. They were a brutal, blood-thirsty gang and there were rewards posted by the three states where they had committed their crimes.

Curtin had shared in that big money, and lost it quickly enough, gambling and generally helling his way around, but it had felt good to be paid for those bitter weeks of posse work. *A lot better than two-fifty a day!*

A hundred dollars now would be fine, but that son of a bitch Spence overlooked one thing: if he was willing to put up a bounty – and that's what it really amounted to – then Owen Jago likely already had a bigger one on this Jared Clay.

And Curtin aimed to claim it.

He made for high country, spurring and lashing his still-fresh claybank. It might be running a dogleg, away from the trail Two Moons had picked up, but Curtin figured it would be worth the extra distance. High ground meant you could see a long way, and a man afoot, staggering and weaving, would stand out against that blinding alkali like a tarantula on a bridal gown.

He knew he had the best horse out of all the posse, and once he spotted Clay he could cut across Two Moons's trail and get to Clay first, no matter how good the damn Injun thought he was.

And there would be no one riding his shoulder to tell him to bring the man in alive.

Jared Clay had to admit he had bitten off more than he could chew with this desert. The alkali was much, much finer than he had ever encountered, seemed to *suck* his boots, hold him back, force him to make more effort to free each foot than he was ready for. More effort meant greater energy loss, more sweat – and one hell of a raging thirst. The water in the canteen was warm, no, more than that, bordering on the *hot*. The blanket covering on the hard-used canteen was worn threadbare, areas ripped off in parts, making the canteen itself clumsy to handle, trying to avoid the sun-heated areas of bare metal. To swallow a mouthful was like drinking from the spout of a coffee pot, but his body cried out for liquid. *Screamed* for it.

In Arizona his father had taught him to think past the desire for thirst: hard efforts requiring constant concentration, but it worked – in some cases. A man had to start out without a thirst for it to work, use his willpower during the gradual onset. But once it took hold and the brain knew it was going to be denied water, then a man was in trouble, real trouble.

Anyway, the times it had worked had been over only short distances. This damn desert seemed to be the entire world now, surrounding him, stretching away in every direction. Even the sky seemed bleached out to the colour of alkali and saltpans. He knew he wasn't coordinating well, the number of times he stumbled or caught himself staggering sideways as if on the reeling deck of a schooner in a big sea. He had never had this happen before and way back in his mind came the notion that maybe this time he *wouldn't* make it across.

It was at the extreme north edge of the massive Devil's Skillet out here and that knowledge told him he was a long way from any green trees and shady pools. If he could find a mountain a thousand feet high he doubted he would be able to see where the desert ended in any direction. . . .

Suddenly, he found himself pushing up frantically on his arms, spitting and clawing hot sand from his face. *Another damn fall!* And he hadn't even noticed it happening!

He sat there, senses dulled, felt a shaft of sudden fear spear through him as he blinked grit and blurring matter from his eyes and cast about frantically.

Where was the canteen?

And his rifle!

The fear shouldered aside the fatigue and lassitude that threatened to engulf him. No water, no means of defence. He dropped a hand quickly and felt some relief when he discovered the Colt was still in its holster, though half buried in sand that had filtered in. He shook it free of grit then lifted a hand – shaking some! – and peeked through his fingers across his eyes, thereby cutting down the glare. He turned slowly, picked up the long wavering line that marked his passage – and a dark blob!

On hands and knees, shaking his hands frequently as he lifted them from the burning sand with each forward thrust, he made his way across – and found the canteen. It had a cork stopper with a metal top attached to a cord so it couldn't be lost. But some of the cork had crumbled away and allowed a good deal of his remaining water to leak. Stifling a curse – he ought to conserve his breath for whatever reason, he figured – he wrapped a corner of his neckerchief around the metal neck so it wouldn't burn his lips and allowed the water to strain through the cloth.

It tasted terrible, but he half-filled his mouth, let it

swill around and gulped it down.

There was no second mouthful. He sucked on the cloth, poked the tip of his swollen tongue into the neck but it was too hot. Upending the canteen, one hand cupped beneath, the found no more than a few drops, which he licked up swiftly, then sat back, the empty container in his lap.

After a while, he picked it up, replaced the faulty stopper, hammering it home with the heel of his hand for no good reason. He wouldn't abandon the vessel: there was always the chance – the *hope!* – that he would find water and he would need something to carry some away with him.

He slung the strap across his upper body, remembered he hadn't found his rifle. To save energy he stayed put, used his finger-slit observation once more and thought he saw a stick – a *straight* stick – lying back along his wavering tracks, maybe ten yards away.

Getting there on hands and knees, the canteen sliding around to his front and entangling his groping hands several times, it felt like ten miles.

He was within six feet of the rifle, for that was the 'stick' he had seen, when suddenly the canteen dangling around his neck clunked and jumped as if kicked by a mule. The strap burned across his neck and shoulder and one arm collapsed under him. His face plunged against the hot sand and he heard the slapping, racketting echo of the shot at the same time as he blinked and saw the bullet hole torn in the metal of the canteen.

Instinct took over.

Wild, desperate instinct, the heart-kicking, primitive urge to survive. His hands didn't even feel the heat of the rifle's stock or the metal of the barrel as he fumbled and levered a shell into the breech. He was rolling away as he did so and saw a spurt of sand an instant before he heard again the crack of the assassin's weapon.

Lean body wrenching around, he was in time to see the gunman riding in, forking a big horse, reins between his teeth, rifle to shoulder. Clay twisted again, rolled as the rider's gun cracked in a rapid volley of three shots that raked the sand around him. Sliding, a small bow-wave of sand building in front of him momentarily, Clay came to a stop and wrestled the rifle butt into his shoudler. He must have jettisoned the riddled canteen because it wasn't there to hinder his movements as he triggered. It was more to let the killer know he was ready to fight back than with any real hope of hitting his target.

The man veered away so suddenly that Clay knew his bullet had gone closer than he could have hoped, and it had scared the killer momentarily. But he was a good horseman and used his knees to bring his claybank back into line, the animal's muscles rippling, glistening with sweat.

The rifle fired but Clay had hurled himself to the right and down a small slope, rolled twice and flopped onto his belly. The rifle settled into his shoulder, the cheekpiece coming in comfortably, except for the trapped sand between the wood and his face, and the sights focused.

The gun jarred twice. The rider leaned slightly from

the saddle as he weaved the claybank, suddenly jerked, groped wildly for the horn, dropping his own rifle. The second bullet took him in the chest and he rolled over the claybank's rump, flopped about on the sand for a few moments and then went still.

Breathing through his mouth, senses spinning, Jared Clay eased his head slowly forward and rested his sunburned forehead on one wrist as he lay there, too weak to move.

The sun hammered his aching brain, and a comforting thought slipped in: with luck, he now had himself a mount.

CHAPTER 9

LONE RIDER

Clay didn't know Curtin's name but he recognized him from town. Not that there was anything he could do for him. That last bullet had snuffed out his life, angling slightly downwards and tearing into his heart.

But the canteen was two-thirds full and he drank a couple of slow mouthfuls, made sure the stopper was well home and carried it with him while he checked things out. The claybank didn't seem all that partial to him, eyed him with suspicion, and Clay noticed some fresh blood on the saddle and the animal's neck from when Curtin had taken his tumble. He wet the end of Curtin's neckerchief and washed away the blood and the horse seemed slightly more amiable then.

There was grub in the saddle-bags, a half-carton of rifle ammunition. He ground-hitched the claybank to make sure it didn't run off, shucked the cartridges from

Curtin's belt and filled the empty loops on his own, putting the remaining shells into his pocket.

He dropped the man's six-shooter into one of the saddle-bags, looked around a little anxiously: that gunfire would have rolled for miles across the desert. A good man could figure the direction right smartly and – *Goddamnit!*

There was a smudge out there already, a long way out, but even as he watched it thickened slightly and spread and he knew the posse was coming.

He looped the canteen strap firmly around the saddlehorn and swung aboard the claybank. It protested, took a casual swipe at his leg to let him know he couldn't expect too much co-operation, and then lunged away in the direction he had been taking before Curtin showed up.

It was still a long, blazing, dry ride out of there and at least some of those posse men would have horses equal to or better than the claybank that showed signs of already having been ridden hard.

In minutes, the heat haze had blurred man and rider, but there was no time to stop and wipe out his tracks.

They would know just where to come, anyway: now it all depended on how fast they came.

Durango Spence turned Curtin over and looked at the two bullet wounds.

'He got it from the front, no bushwhack.'

'Thought he was goin' back to town,' someone wondered.

Spence nodded, taking off his hat and shaking alkali from it in a cloud that made him cough. 'Curtin bein' Curtin – always a stubborn coot – likely figured he'd nail Clay, put himself up to claim any reward Jago's got riding on him.'

Two Moons straightened from where he had been examining the tracks. Hands on hips he looked off into the thickening heat haze. He chopped a hand through the throat-rasping air.

'That way. Curtin's hoss good. We got hard ride to make, Durango.'

Spence nodded. 'OK. Pete, you and Kip bury Curtin, then come on. We're goin' after Clay right now.'

The two posse men chosen for the burial detail weren't too happy; apart from the work, it meant they might lose the chance of claiming the $100 Spence was offering for the first sighting and apprehension of Jared Clay.

There was broken country ahead. Low, stark, desolate, standing out even in this bleak landscape. Low, ragged ridges like a line of broken sawteeth, none higher than thirty feet.

Not much advantage, but every little concession was welcome, Clay thought as he put the claybank between the first of the eroded hillocks: they looked like something an artist would paint if he wanted to convey a mood of total despair. *Ridges and shadows, like ribs pushing against stretched skin.*

He shook his throbbing head: the heat and the long strain of being on the run were getting to him. His mind was spinning and he had to fight to stay concentrated. Stopping the panting horse, the foam drying and caking in yellowish streaks on its dusty hide, he stood in the stirrups, feeling his legs quivering. His knee nudged the canteen and water sloshed enticingly, but he clamped his scaled lips tightly, shaded his eyes and scanned his backtrail.

He swore. That dust cloud was much closer now, so close he could make out the dark shapes of the riders beneath. They had made good time. He had hoped they would stop to bury the dead man but likely had left someone to do that chore while the rest rode along his trail. He had spotted the Indian tracker long ago and had thought of stopping at that time, and picking the man off.

Now he wished he had.

The posse was coming straight for these hummocks: he couldn't think of them as real hills because they were so low. They were eroded by the endless winds, still looked like the ribcages of dead men when the sun threw shadows from the raised ridges.

Man! He had better watch it! His mind was leaning much too frequently towards depressing thoughts!

'Damn it!' he muttered, unslung the canteen and took a long swallow. Dehydration made a man's mind conjure up some weird thoughts. Anyway, if he was going to die, he didn't aim to leave this corner of hell for the real thing, thirsty.

That was the first he realized he had already subconsciously made up his mind to make a stand here. The old brain wasn't as sluggish as he had figured, he reckoned, as he dismounted, rolled a heat-cracked rock over the trailing rein ends and just missed being bitten on the shoulder by the protesting claybank. Instinctively, he slapped it with his hat.

Then, contrite, he gave the animal some water from the crushed-in crown of that same hat.

By then, some eager beaver in the posse tried a long shot. It was beyond the rifle's range but they were coming in fast now, spreading out, closing off his possible escape routes: the way Spence spread his men, they could cover both ends and the middle, cooping him up in these lousy dry ridges.

Spence was smart: he stopped the posse just out of rifle range, using field glasses to scan the low hills, searching for Clay's position and, of course, trying to draw his fire.

Clay obliged him, using the Vernier scale flip-up rear sight. But it had been damaged, the base pin bent, canting the scale when he flipped it to the vertical. He fired anyway, the bullet making a puff of dust some yards to the left and well in front of the sheriff.

He cursed soflty. He would have to rely on the regular v-sight, which meant firing at a closer range. He had done enough shooting to judge elevation for a far-reaching shot, but the accuracy would be suspect in this glare.

Draw them in! That was the only way, but there were six of them, and two riders coming in, likely the ones who had been on burial detail. Hell, he had never been much for killing, man or animal. He had done both, of course, and would do it again when he had to, but all he wanted now was to get away. He didn't want to leave a trail of dead men or he would never know peace again, never be able to settle down anywhere, and there would be bounties on his head that many a man would figure was worth the effort of tracking him down and putting a bullet in his back.

When the dodger said 'Dead or Alive' it meant only 'dead', and it didn't matter how.

Spence must have figured he could cover this area of broken ridges with the number of men he had under his control. He held a short conference, waved his arms and the men spread out in a longer line, an arc, this time, the outer men covering both ends of the tangle of hills. Four men were backing Durango Spence as they prepared to charge.

Clay swore. He was going to have to kill some good horseflesh here and knock a few riders out of their saddles if he aimed to make his getaway.

Spence's voice reached him faintly, though not the exact words. Not that it mattered: the man's gestures said everything as he waved his men forward and the ragged line of riders lifted their mounts' reins, raked with the spurs.

And just as the charge started, there was a thudding of gunfire, three evenly-spaced shots, that reached the posse's ears a moment before Clay himself heard it.

He straightened from taking his first sight down the hot barrel of his Winchester, eased the tightening of his finger on the trigger.

A lone rider was racing in towards the posse, his arm lifted. There were three more spaced shots: drawing

100

attention to him as h fired his six-gun into the air.

'What the—'

The posse had reined down and most of their guns were trained on the rider as he kept coming. Spence held up a hand in an unnecessary gesture as the horses snorted and pranced, wishing the damn riders would make up their minds what they wanted them to do.

Crouching, Clay watched as the rider skidded his mount to a halt before Durango Spence. He could tell by the sheriff's stiff shoulders and the way he thrust his head forward that he was angrily demanding to know what the hell this interloper wanted?

Jared Clay would dearly like to know himself.

For a few minutes he watched as the newcomer spoke with Spence, saw the lawman turn his head twice to look towards where he knew Clay to be. The posse men seemed animated and excited, their horses restless under their riders, until Spence apparently told them to shut up. He questioned the new rider intently, took off his hat and slapped it across his thighs, scratching his head as he turned his gaze one more time to the ridges.

Clay had slid out of sight now, taking advantage of the posse's distraction to change position. But he could still see them as he stretched out between two cracked rocks, holding his rifle ready, but not allowing the barrel to show and give him away.

Then his eyes widened and he straightened, despite himself, his hat showing above the rock. He ducked swiftly but he needn't have bothered.

Spence, the posse, and the lone rider were leaving,

riding away from the bleak, broken ridges, heading back the way they had come, in the direction of Barton Falls.

Clay simply sat there and stared, waiting for something to wake him from what he figured had to be a dream, some illusion brought on by stress and heat and thirst.

But it was no dream.

That lone rider had been a townsman named Chet Bidell and he had been sent to find Spence and the posse as fast as he could.

The news he had given them had been simple – and surprising.

Lonnie Cousins had rallied, might still die, but he had been lucid long enough to tell Doc Bateson and Ella that Jared Clay had not tried to kill him. Clay had left by the time Hal Getty came round and savagely beat up on Cousins, in an attempt to learn where the keys to the office safe were kept so he could open it and take the gold nuggets that were in there.

'So, Clay ain't the man you want,' Chet Bidell told the disappointed Durango Spence. 'Getty's the son of a bitch who smashed up Lonnie Cousins an' left him for dead.'

The sheriff's face reflected the anger and disappointment he felt, but he had always been a tolerably fair man, if mighty hard at times.

Looking up at the broken ridges, glimpsing Clay's hat just showing above a line of rocks, he growled,

'All right. Back to town. Then we'll see if we can pick up this Getty's tracks.'

'You gonna tell Clay?' a man asked.

'Let him find out for himself. Anyway, beyond those ridges is the south-west line of Brazos County. I'd chase a killer over there, hell or high water, but if he's just runnin' from the chain gang, the hell with it. Clay and them other prisoners did damn good work in Waco, helpin' out after the twister, so mebbe he deserves a break. Anyway, that's Jago's country. He can have him now. *Come on!*'

Puzzled and incredulous, Clay watched the posse ride away, not knowing why he had gotten this sudden reprieve, but he aimed to take full advantage of it.

Fatigue overwhelmed Clay in the afternoon. It had been a long, hot ride through Hell. He was sure Old Nick's place couldn't be any hotter or drier than this Skillet desert. He had been fighting thirst, the urge to drink plaguing him as the claybank made its way down out of the ridges and onto the blazing white glare of the alkali. He didn't know how far yet he had to travel to get clear of this desolation and, with the experience of many other desert crossings, he conserved his water supply. Deep down he knew – *hoped,* anyway – that he had more than enough water to see him through so he could hold out for long periods without a drink as long as he knew one was there when he absolutely needed it.

That was the killer out here. A man with a mighty thirst upon him, not knowing when the next drop of moisture would pass his lips, began to give up, whether he was aware of it or not.

His organs started to dry out, the skin felt like paper,

not safe to rub or scratch in case it came away and exposed raw flesh, the tongue began to swell, and by that time panic had well and truly set in. He was suffering all these physical discomforts but behind the dizziness and nausea and general feeling of fast-encroaching disability was the knowledge that once he decided he couldn't bear it any longer, he could still reach for the canteen and swallow a mouthful, a *life-giving* mouthful.

Without that safety factor he knew he wouldn't make it.

But right now he was close to grabbing the sloshing canteen, didn't believe he could stand that tantalizing liquid splashing any longer.

Suddenly, there was a bright yellow flash behind his eyes and he thought someone had shone a mirror into his face. But it was his slowly dehydrating brain, still working through the growing lethargy, warning him he may not be alone, to take necessary precautions, like watching his backtrail.

It took a good deal of effort to physically wrench around in the saddle, red, mattery eyes squinting as he scanned a 180-degree arc.

Hell! He couldn't even see clearly! A damn war-party of Indians could be closing in for all he could tell.

'*Slow down, Clay!*'

The words hit him like an open-handed slap, and he hauled rein, heaving upright in the saddle, sure he heard his aching bones creak. Hot breath searing his dried-out nostrils, he dropped a hand to his six-gun's staghorn grips.

104

'Leave it!'

He moved his head towards the voice now. It was close, only a few yards away. He could make out the shadowy outline of a rider sitting his mount across his path. A dull flash had to be sunlight striking gunmetal but he couldn't yet tell if he was covered by six-gun or rifle.

Despite the man's order he let his hand stay gripping the butt of his Colt.

'You from the posse?' Clay was surprised at how much effort it took for him to talk, the roughness and depth of his voice.

'No posse. You must've seen 'em back off. Spence himself led 'em back to the Falls.'

He knew who it was now! Recognized that suspicious, 'don't-mess-with me' voice.

'Getty!'

'Right. Don't think it makes you lucky. I heard enough from my hidin' place to know Cousins wasn't quite dead an' he told 'em it was me smashed his head in and so on.'

Clay frowned, the very presence of danger alerting his whole, suffering body now. 'Why'd you do that?'

'Wanted the gold in the damn law office safe but the son of a bitch wouldn't tell me where the key was. Then Spence arrived so I said was you beat up on Cousins.'

'Thanks a lot, you slimy bastard!'

'Look, I don't mind killin' you, Clay. I've struck out twice, it seems, not finishin' ol' Mose Tatum, or Cousins, but I'll finish you when I'm good and ready. That's gospel. But for now, you ain't wanted for murder or even attempted murder. *I'm* the unlucky sonuver they want! But that's OK. 'Cause now you're gonna tell me where Mose found them nuggets, or you'll show me. Them's your choices.'

'Kill me and you won't ever find out whether I really know where to find the gold or not.'

He could see much better now he had turned half-on to the sun, and he saw Getty's eyes narrow.

'You don't get it, do you? I got no choice I *have* to believe Mose told you. There ain't no other way of me ever findin' out the location. Whether he told you or not ain't gonna make any difference to you, though. I'm gonna put you through some things'd make an Apache puke. And if you finally die without tellin' me, then that's it.' He grinned crookedly. 'But you'll be the winner, you know? Because you'll be almighty glad to die, *happy* to do it just to end what I got planned for you.'

The rifle barrel jerked in a short arc.

'Climb on down an' let's get started, with any luck I'll be on my way to that gold before sun-up . . . and you'll be in Hell!'

CHAPTER 10

AN OLD ENEMY

It was clear that Getty had been here before. He knew an easy way out of the ridges, down in the bottom of the 'rib cages' where the ground was surprisingly firm, yet cushioned the hoofs, deadening much of the sound.

He seemed more confident as they rode on into the afternoon. Surreptitiously studying the slant of the sun as it dropped slowly into the west, Clay figured they were headed north of west, which would put them . . . *where?*

In the distance was a low smudge of grey with a suggestion of green here and there and some other dull, faded indeterminate colour. A line of hills, beyond the desert's edge, if that green meant anything. Not only that, the silhouette of the rims, as far as he could make out, had a vaguely familiar pattern.

A man whose life was, or had been, one long drift

across and around the country, noted things a normal traveller might not. The ranges had distinctive features. Up close it might be a spilled basalt scar down the slope of the second northernmost mountain; or trees with a defiinite lean in the direction of a wind powerful enough to bend them that way; or an old landslide could have left a big slice gnawed out of the slope like the edge of a rotten tooth; or, as was common, and this was a sign Clay always looked for when approaching a new range, the pattern of the sawtoothed crests.

He might be hard put to describe the exact lay of the undulation of a particular range, but he would know it instantly if he saw it, even from miles away, and years later.

And he knew the pattern on that distant, low-lying range beyond the desert. He couldn't be absolutely certain from this distance, with his eyes heat-blasted, the glare, and the low level of the range itself, but he was pretty certain he recognized those hills.

In sudden defiance, catching Getty off guard, he snatched his canteen from the horn where it hung on its strap and took several large swallows of water before the killer could ride in and ram his horse hard into the claybank. The animal whickered and, being a feisty mount, bit at Getty's horse and blood flowed. Big teeth bared. Whinnies shrilled.

The horses tangled and Getty looked startled at what he had precipitated, swung his rifle barrel at Clay, who, prior to grabbing the canteen, had been drooping listlessly in the saddle, moaning as if pain.

So, Hal Getty was mighty surprised when Clay not

only ducked deftly under the swinging rifle barrel, but came up beneath it, grabbed it and yanked. Getty came out of the saddle, at the last moment getting a bit of leverage on the stirrup irons. So he hit Clay harder than expected and both men crashed to the ground. The horses snorted and sorted themselves out, prancing away from the rolling, scuffling men. The rifle was lost somewhere during their kicking and elbowing. Clay took a boot on the right shoulder and went sprawling on his back.

Getty threw himself on top of him – or started to. But he ran into a pair of lifted riding boots that took him in the chest and slammed the breath out of him. He tried to roll away but lost co-ordination briefly and slid onto his face. Clay kicked him in the side, came up to his knees and overbalanced when he took a swing at Getty's head.

Hal Getty's fists pounded, hammering, driving against Clay's head and neck, forcing him to duck and cover, using his forearms. He dodged and weaved, felt a blow scrape his left ear as the fist just missed and slid over his shoulder. He straightened swiftly, ramming that arm up, forcing Getty off balance. His right whistled around and cracked against Getty's jaw.

The man's legs slid out from under him and he went down, but rolled and skidded as he slid a few feet down the slope. Then he reared to his knees, reaching for his Colt.

He had taken Clay's six-gun before they had started the ride through the ridges. Now Clay saw his horse had decided discretion was the better part of valour, dodged away from the bigger animal, sliding towards him. He jumped for it and Getty lifted his aim, shooting quickly, but missing.

By then Clay had ripped open the flap on the saddle-bag, reached in and found his own old six-gun he had placed there earlier when he decided to keep Curtin's Colt. The claybank was still sliding and Getty threw himself aside, trying for another shot. Clay triggered, shooting through the saddle-bag, causing the horse to whinny and lunge away wildly.

All of which threw Getty's concentration and then Clay's Colt came free of the bag and he dropped smoothly to one knee, triggering twice, steadying his gunhand with an elbow on the raised knee and tight grip from his left hand.

Getty spun with the bullet's impact: the first had missed but the second slammed home, knocking him down into a ten-foot slide. By the time he had come to a halt, dust boiling around him, Clay was bounding down, fell and rolled against the wounded man. He pressed the hot gun muzzle under Getty's slack jaw, pain-glazed eyes meeting his cold gaze.

'Now. Let's you and me have that palaver, Getty. Only this time, maybe it'll be you praying to die fast and get it over with. Savvy?'

Getty was all through, demoralized. Clay's bullet had smashed his right collarbone and there is hardly another bone in the human body that can produce as much sheer, unmitigated agony when shattered.

He had a period of screaming, then sobbing, even

pleading. Clay wasn't ignorant of the man's suffering but there was very little he could do. Still, he made a kind of harness-sling from the spare harness he was able to put together from both their horses and the accompanying saddle-gear. Getty had a spare shirt in his saddle-bag and this was torn up, padded, the remaining cloth laced in the armpit to help ease the strain on the broken shoulder. Of course, Getty passed out the instant Clay started to try to align the broken ends of the bones. He gave up on it quickly enough. There was no point in Getty suffering something that was only an amateurish attempt anyway, and a not very successful one at that. So he arranged it as well as he could while Getty was unconscious, although the man still writhed and moaned, adjusted his harness, with the pockets torn from Getty's pants and partly filled with sand. This gave them body and flexibility and prevented the leather rubbing or moving too much, which would only aggravate the wound.

He took another swallow from the dwindling amount of water left in the canteen, held the neck against Getty's lips. The man, still out to it, swallowed automatically, greedily. But he only had a taste. Clay stood up, capping the bottle, looking down at the wounded man. With his ghastly colour and all the blood spattered around, he could have been dead. But air whistled and honked raggedly through his nostrils and mouth.

'Now how the hell am I gonna get you onto your hoss and into a sawbones?' he mused half aloud.

'Mebbe I can lend a hand.'

111

Clay whirled, his Colt coming up but he froze as he looked down the muzzle of a Winchester, held rock steady by Durango Spence. The sheriff jerked the barrel and Clay let his gun slide back into leather.

'You spend more time treatin' the men you shoot than tryin' to get away, Clay. No, don't get up. Just stay squatting like you are.'

'Way I hear it, I don't have to dodge any posses now.'

Spence's dusty, weary face straightened. 'Well, Lonnie cleared you of tryin' to kill him but he died just before we got back to town.' He looked a mite wistful. 'My sister's boy. Lost her husband . . . well, be honest, they never married . . . but she had to rear Lonnie by herself. I lent a hand when I could. He weren't bad, was turning into a pretty good lawman, when this son of a bitch' – he gestured to Getty with the rifle – 'cut his life short.' He looked like he might kick the wounded killer but Durango Spence was more man than that. 'I got a reward put out on his head before I came after him. Town Council came up with $2,000, more'n I expected, but then Lonnie had kept a good safe town.'

Clay's head jerked at the amount of the reward.

'Am I eligible to claim it?'

Spence frowned. 'You nailed him, so I guess so, but we're in Owen Jago's county here. I was on my way to pay him the courtesy of lettin' him know I'd be hunting down Getty in his bailiwick when I heard the shootin'. Looks like we'll have to get this scum into town and doctored up. I aim to see him swing – all nice and legal.'

Clay looked at him steadily. 'How about me?'

'You? I already decided you done some good work in

Waco. I know of Ryker and I don't doubt he was capable of framin' you for rustlin' to get you off that land. Likely would've killed you except he's leery of Jago. And you've done a heap of hard time already. Far as I'm concerned, if you get away, then good luck to you.'

'If I get away. That mean I'm your prisoner right now?'

'Means we got a heap of ridin' to do before dark.' He gestured to the long smudged line of hills. 'It'll take the two of us to get him into town.'

'Dunno that I want to go near any town. Specially one with Owen Jago as sheriff.'

Spence's eyes were expressionless. 'We'll see. But right now, I'm calling the tune. Let's get under way.'

They made night camp among sparse green trees scat+ tered around a waterhole not much bigger than a rooming-house bath tub. It was tea-coloured with layers of dead leaves on the bottom and tasted strongly of tannin but it was mighty welcome to the trio.

Spence was well equipped for his manhunt and hadn't even touched his supplies before he rode in on Clay and the wounded Getty. So they brewed coffee from fresh-ground beans. It wasn't top-notch but went down well, and Spence even produced a flat bottle of whiskey and laced their drinks. He spilled a goodly amount into Getty's, held the back of the man's head while letting him drink.

Hal Getty's eyes were droopy-lidded, filled with pain, but they showed some life as he looked from the sheriff to Clay.

113

'Damndest spot I ever been in, shot an' doctored by one of you, fed spiked java by the law.'

'How's the shoulder?' Clay asked and Getty merely grimaced.

'We'll have a sawbones fix you up,' Spence told him flatly. 'Good enough so's you'll stand trial.'

Getty merely nodded: it was clear there was no more fight left in the man. He knew whatever happened he would never have full use of that arm again. Or maybe he'd swing and wouldn't have to worry about that part at all.

'Ryker's to blame,' Getty said bitterly into the silence that developed while they ate fresh-baked biscuits with slices of cold beef.

Jared Clay snapped his head up. 'Kit Ryker? Circle R?'

Getty nodded slightly, muttered an obscenity prefixed to Ryker's name. 'Worked for him, little over a year back. Or worked for a survey company. Mightn't look it but I started out as a surveyor. We were mappin' around that area of them Runnin' Dog Hills, got friendly with some of the Circle R crew. Usual enough when you're camped on ranch land for a few weeks. Feller named Sundeen started bringin' us beefsteaks and so on, got real friendly, brought a little booze and loosened our tongues, I guess. I must've told him I had some gamblin' debts to pay off and they were worryin' me. He took me up to meet Ryker, who offered me money, a thousand bucks, to run my survey line t'other side of a creek which would bring water and the mighty good pasture surrounding it onto Circle R land.'

114

'Who owned the land at that time?'

Getty shrugged. 'Was classed as "open range" but our job was to map all the so-called free range and bring it onto the Government books. Had been too many feuds and range wars over such land. The Agency aimed to label every inch and mark the boundaries so there'd be no more squabbles. Gov'ment could point to the map and say that land or this belongs to whoever, or maybe just Gov'ment, an' hope that'd settle things.'

Clay nodded. 'That's how come that land went up as a prove-up quarter-section. It's the one I was workin' when Ryker framed me for rustling his maverick.'

Getty arched his eyebrows and the effort it cost him to do so was noticeable. Spence was mighty interested and motioned for the wounded man to continue. It was taking a lot out of Getty but the man seemed to want to get it off his chest.

'There was a foul-up. Chief Surveyor noticed my readings were off, fired me on the spot. Ryker had already paid me the money after I said I'd done what he wanted so I had to clear out, pronto. But Sundeen and someone called Longo caught up with me, beat me up. I'd gambled most of the money and they said I'd better pay Ryker back or they'd catch up with me and cripple me for life. Not kill me, but bust up my legs an' spine so's I'd never walk again, but have plenty of pain.'

Spence glanced at Clay. 'Sound like Ryker?'

'Not sure. Sounds like Sundeen and Longo, though.'

'I said I could get the money, broke away from 'em. I'd made friends with old Tatum before then and knew he was headed into the desert. So I went after him and more or less forced myself on him as a pardner. I figured a hatful of gold nuggets was the best way of gettin' Ryker off my neck, but. . . .' He paused, gasping for breath by now, laid his eyes on Clay. 'Well, you know what happened, an' how I ended up here.'

Neither Spence nor Clay said anything and Getty added, obviously wondering if he had done the right thing admitting his wrongs, 'I din' mean to kill Cousins, not even hurt him much, I just wanted the key to the safe. If I coulda gotten my hands on them nuggets. I was desperate by then. Guess I got carried away. I'm truly sorry, Spence.'

'You think what the nuggets are worth would've satisfied Ryker?' Clay asked dubiously.

'Guess not. But it would've stalled him long enough for me to make another run for it. Or mebbe I thought they could be a getaway stash for me.'

Clay and the lawman remained silent. Eventually, Getty passed out again. Clay rolled a cigarette and handed the makings to the sheriff.

'Just greedy, looking for easy money,' he opined.

'That's the way it goes with most of 'em,' Spence agreed. 'He's sorry now he's been caught, but fact is, he backshot old Tatum and messed-up Lonnie bad enough to kill him. He's gonna hang.' Handing back the tobacco sack, he looked into Clay's face. 'With your testimony.'

'Wait a minute! I ain't going anywhere near Owen Jago or no court! You got Getty's confessionn.'

'Needs corroboration, which means you.'

Clay swore. 'All I wanted was to prove-up on that

quarter-section. I've had a helluva lot of aggravation ever since, some of it caused by you. Now I'm almost back where I started, except I'm still a fugitive, and you want me to square up to a law court?' He shook his head, made to put the tobacco sack in his shirt pocket and suddenly his Colt was in his hand and Spence was rearing upright, cigarette hanging from his lower lip.

'Now take it easy!'

'This is as far as I go, Spence: you've got Lonnie's killer. Said yourself you didn't figure I had much to answer for. Now stick by that and I'll just ride out of here and you'll never see me again.'

'I want Getty to swing!'

'Any jury'll find him guilty.'

'Crippled with that arm, lookin' the way he does, like he's been dragged through hell, contrite, gets that "done-me-wrong" whine in his voice? Christ, he gets a good lawyer and they could hang *me*!'

'Then take your chances, but I'm not coming with you.'

'Listen, Clay, I can see you're a decent enough *hombre*. How am I gonna get Getty into a sawbones without your help?'

Clay waved the gun briefly. 'There's timber here, saplings. Make a *travois*.'

Spence's eyes narowed. 'You son of a bitch! You got an answer for everythin', don't you?'

'No. But you've had my answer on this.'

Spence heaved a sigh. 'All right. Will you write out a statement, layin' out Getty's story, an' sign it? That'll help.'

Clay hesitated, then nodded. 'But I tie you up first.'

'Jesus! What about the reward for capturing Getty? You gonna pass that up?'

'If it stands between me and staying free, I am.' Spence shook his head. 'Tell you what. Pay the money to Janet Horton. She runs the J Bar H. I sort of owe her a favour. I got your word on that?'

'You're plumb loco! Like everyone I've knowed from Arizona! All them deserts must dehydrate your brains or somethin'! But OK, you got my word, damn you.'

'All right. Just roll over onto your belly and put your hands behind your back.'

'What if I don't? You won't shoot! Not your style.'

'My style is to stay free. I may not shoot you, but I'll give you a headache that feels like every hangover you've ever had rolled into one.'

He made a brief, cutting motion with the gun barrel and Spence glared bleakly, then rolled over, putting his hands behind his back.

'An' just as I was beginnin' to like you, Clay!'

'Aw, shucks, you're making me blush. How's that? Not too tight?'

CHAPTER 11

NIGHT FIRE

Spence would be able to wriggle out of his bonds without too much trouble: Clay had tied them that way. But by that time, Clay aimed to be far away in the darkness, using the brilliant edge-of-desert stars to guide him where he wanted to go.

And that was out of here, a *long* way out of here, beyond the reach of Owen Jago, Spence or anyone else – and likely that could include Ryker. The man wasn't likely to forget what Clay's headbutt had done to change his face and, being a vain man to start with, knowing Clay was on the loose would set Ryker's rage boiling anew.

So he swung to the north the trail Spence had been riding, and figured this would take him away from Jago, the Circle R and Brazos County in general. He wasn't sure whether he would clear every ranch in this neck of the woods but he could always wait until dark if he thought he was going to be exposed too much by crossing cattle pastures in daylight.

He was weary and full of aches right into the marrow of his bones from the desert crossing and all his efforts before that. It would be good to find a quiet little hideaway where he could rest up for a couple of days before making his final run out of this neck of the woods.

He thought about where his present trail was going to take him: close to his original prove-up quarter-section – *That dream had crashed long ago, so forget it, put it down to experience.* He wondered if Lew Allison had made the deadline, and if he had, would he have sold the land to Ryker by now? Not that it mattered one way or another now.

They were just thoughts to occupy him as the time passed, but he knew he wasn't going to make it through the night without rest. Using the star scatter as a background, he studied the undulations of the ranges he was now travelling through. His eyes weren't good enough yet, after all that desert glare, to be sure, but he thought he recognized a slope two hills across from where he was riding.

Somewhere back of Circle R – no, likely closer to the Horton girl's place – but he had hunted mule deer there and knew there was a pleasant little valley between the hills, with a small stream, too small to be called a creek. But there was good grass and both he and the claybank could rest a spell for the daylight hours, move out again tomorrow night before moonrise.

That appealed to him and he took a few rough bearings that would lead him down and across, after a small swing south-east, over a close-in hogback.

It was from the crest of this small rise that he saw the bright flare briefly illuminating some brush – and the big hand with the leather wrist-cuff holding the match flame to a bundle of sticks.

The flames blossomed as the dry sticks ignited and he saw the man holding them clearly.

He should have known by the leather cuffs it was Brack Longo. The flames showed the Circle R man clearly now, running towards what looked like a wall of brush only yards away. He skidded to a stop, hurled his blazing torch.

It was a brush fence, stretched across the narrow entrance to a small draw, bushes lashed to a rough sapling frame to form a gate. And, as it flared, he heard the first frightened bellowing of cattle in the draw itself.

'*Judas Priest! It was a holding draw!*' Rounded-up mavericks, most likely, held here at a gathering point and when there were enough, or no more worth collecting, they would be driven down to the main pastures . . . *where?*

There was only one ranch this draw could belong to: Janet Horton's J Bar H.

And Longo was probably following orders from Kit Ryker to destroy the imprisoned herd.

Even as these thoughts galloped through his mind, awakening his senses, starting the adrenalin flowing, he spurred the claybank up the slope, riding out of a heavy blanket of darkness that, as a background, would make

121

him hard to see. The roaring and crackling of the flames, not to mention the now frantic bawling of the trapped steers, would prevent Longo from hearing his approach.

But not entirely.

Longo heard something, himself a clear target now in the red light of the fire. He drew his gun, crouching, jumping back into shadows. But as the flames took hold the light washed over the slope like a flooding tide and Longo had to keep on the move, trying to stay ahead of it.

But he was silouetted against the fire he had started, and he only realized this when Clay's rifle stabbed flame out of the blackness and bullets whistled past him. He dropped flat, rolling, a man of violent action, a quick-thinking veteran of many gunfights. He flopped onto his belly, ramming his gun-arm elbow into the soft earth to steady his aim, triggered three fast shots at Clay's charging figure. He rolled instantly and jumped up, running towards his horse. Clay heard the lead and the claybank faltered briefly, grunting, winged perhaps, but how seriously he would have to wait to find out.

He wheeled the straining animal towards Longo as the man leapt from rock to rock, making for his own mount, now tugging and wrenching, wild-eyed, at its reins that were tied to a bush near the blazing gate. Red sparks showered down out of the night around it, searing its hide, bringing whinnies of brief pain and anger as the nostrils flared.

Clay rode Longo down.

He slammed the horse into the running man as

Longo pounded towards his own mount, six-gun empty now. The claybank hit the Circle R man and hurled him, flailing, several feet. He crashed into a rock and dropped to his knees, dazed. But he was a fighting man and ignored the pain after the first wave, lunged up and grabbed for the butt of his rifle, poking out of the under-leg saddle scabbard he favoured.

The gun slid out of leather as Longo threw himself backward, levering before he touched the ground, spinning and firing one-handed. The rifle barrel jumped and the shot missed. He brought the gun across his chest as the claybank loomed above him and Clay leaned down and smashed his own rifle barrel across the man's head. Ryker's hardcase fell unconscious and Clay swept on to the blazing brush fence. He could see the sapling frame now as the thick, tied-on brush burned away. He could also see the wild, white eyes of the stomping, bawling cattle as they crowded up to the far end of the draw, getting as far away from the flames as they could.

He unshipped his rope, tossed a loop over a frame upright, then made a fast smooth dally around the saddlehorn. He wrenched the prancing horse around, digging in with the spurs.

The claybank needed no urging to lunge away, paused, strained, and then there was a series of cracks as the sapling frame snapped. The drag of the remains of the gate almost halted the horse, but it was a powerful animal and wanted to get away from the fire.

Clay dropped the rope and spurred the horse around the blazing frame into the draw where grass and brush was also burning.

He came in at a slant to the bunched cattle, saw they were on the verge of stampede. He jumped the claybank behind some low rocks, triggered three shots into the air and that was all that was needed to set them running.

The herd surged by, snorting, bawling, horns clashing, running out of the entrance and veering away from the dying flames on the gate frame.

Longo, dazed, was just staggering up when the first line of steers crashed into him.

He didn't make a sound as the panic-driven hoofs pulped his hard-muscled body, trampling it into the soft earth.

Being a range man from way back, and knowing the danger of fire in cattle country, Jared Clay, though staggering with fatigue, wrenched a green bush from the earth and, neckerchief tied over his lower face, slapped and kicked and pounded at the tufts of grass and clumps of bush that still burned, scattered throughout the miniature canyon.

It was tiring, and the heat that was contained by the draw's walls beat back at him like some giant fist, sucking from him what little hydration his body had retained these past days.

Dizziness overtook him and he collapsed to hands and knees, saw there were still a few small fires, but he was too weak now to do anything about them.

He slumped back against a charred deadfall, and the singed bush he had been using sagged into his lap, his fingers curled loosely about the stem.

He knew he was passing out but could do nothing about it, feeling consciousness drain from him as if someone had pulled a plug.

A J Bar H cowboy named Simm Barry was the first to find him in the grey light of early morning.

The sun's rays hadn't yet penetrated into these hills and the contrast between the patches of light and the jet-black shadows was confusing. But Simm was able to make out the living man from the trampled pile of raw meat a few yards away. He gulped, skirted what was left of Longo, recognizing one torn and broken forearm with the scuffed leather protective cuff still in place on the broken wrist.

Avoiding looking that way, gun drawn, he climbed up the slope to where Clay sagged awkwardly against the charred deadfall. He tore down the neckerchief, wasn't sure if he recognized him or not. Then he stood and triggered three spaced shots into the early morning air, sending clouds of protesting birds screeching out of the treetops and brush.

Simm, a cowboy in his early forties, sat down and waited, occasionally looking at Clay who was stirring slowly now.

Riders appeared down the slope, two men and a woman. They saw Simm, waved, and set their mounts up. Janet Horton was the first to quit leather and hurry forward to stare at Clay, after a quick – very quick – glance towards Longo.

'Aren't you Jared Clay?' A morning zephyr stirred

her long hair and she pushed it irritably away from her face as the dishevelled Clay squinted at her.

He nodded, voice raspy, throat raw from all the smoke. 'Howdy, ma'am. Nice to see you again.'

'What's happened here?' she demanded, frowning. 'Part of a herd we had cooped up here straggled into home pastures, most with scorched hides. I can see why. How did the fire start?'

Between gasps and gulps of water from a canteen one of the cowboys handed him, Clay told her.

'I found Longo's hoss, too, ma'am,' Simm Barry said quietly. 'Two empty coal oil bottles in his saddle-bags. He come up here to burn them cows alive.'

Her hazel eyes flicked towards the grisly pile a few yards away. 'That's Longo?'

Clay nodded. 'He didn't get out of the way fast enough.'

Her frown deepened. 'He was afoot?'

Again Clay nodded. 'I rode him down. He was shooting at me.'

'See your claybank's got a bullet burn across one side of the chest,' allowed Simm Barry. 'Ain't serious, though.'

The girl pursed her lips. 'Ryker has been forcing things more and more lately. I . . . I guess this was just one more way to hassle me. He knew we'd scoured the hills for mavericks and we were getting ready to brand.'

Clay looked puzzled. 'That's range war stuff.'

'It is. Like cut fences that allow my stock animals access to loco weed and quagmires. Or men sent to town on errrands suddenly involved in drunken brawls and hurt badly enough to need medical attention, and when they recover they suddenly decide to quit . . . or maybe next time there won't be any recovery.'

'What's Jago doing about this? He's s'posed to be the hotshot lawman around these parts, ain't he?'

'He is, and a stickler for dotting i's and crossing t's as you ought to know. If there isn't any actual proof, he won't act. Oh, he's warned Ryker many a time, in the manner of, "If someone's stupid enough to stir up a range war they can expect no mercy from me". All well and good, and sincere enough, but not really much of a deterrrent. Ryker's sending me broke, with all these fences to repair, losing stock to loco weed—'

'It'll work out, ma'am.'

'I wish I had your confidence!'

'Well, there's enough of Longo left to back up this deal. Burns to his hands, and Simm says there's coal oil bottles in his gear. Jago can't ignore those things.'

Janet glanced involuntarily towards the victim of the stampede and quickly looked back to Clay.

'But will it prove how he died? Or that he set fire to the fence? Deliberately tried to kill my herd?'

'He'll have my testimony—' Clay stopped even as she began to shake her head slowly.

'I can't allow you to stick your neck out for me any further, Clay. You're still a fugitive, remember. Jago won't forget that. Not that he wouldn't like to accept the evidence, but he runs a tight ship, as he's fond of saying. If he's convinced a man's guilty, and has the evidence to prove it, he'll prosecute to the limit of the law and show no mercy. By the same token, if there isn't sufficient evidence to take to court, he'll feel obligated to give the accused man the benefit of the doubt until he investigates further.'

Clay nodded slowly. 'I've heard about him for years and what you say adds up to the picture I've had of Jago – and what I saw of him at my trial.'

'What we gonna do now, Jan?' asked Simm. 'Won't be able to use this place for a long time . . . not enough grass left to hide a snake.'

'Which is what Ryker wants,' she snapped bitterly. 'The fire has destroyed the feed and if some or most of the herd had been killed at the same time. . . . It's still a big delay.' She glanced at Clay. 'Our lower pastures are still waterlogged after the torrential rains. I have to keep my cattle on the higher slopes. Apart from a scarcity of grass, there are the predators – and not just mountain lions and wolves, there are two-legged predators, too.'

Simm had rolled Clay a cigarette and the man nodded his thanks, dipped the end into the match flame.

'Is Ryker all-out agin you now? Wanting to take over J Bar H?'

'Wanting to take over the entire county. Circle R and J Bar H combined would be an area as large as some European kingdoms. The man who owns them would wield a tremendous amount of power, and could call the tune when it came time to elect a town council, a mayor, or a new sheriff.'

'Never knew he was that ambitious.'

'I think he has been all along, but since you left, his

young sister in San Antonio has married the son of a Congressman. Do I need to go on?'

Clay blew smoke and shook his head. 'You've got a passel of trouble landing in your lap.'

She smiled ruefully. 'Think I don't know it? But come on back to the ranch and you can get cleaned up. And there'll be a bunk for you. You look absolutely worn out.'

'I'll go along with that . . . and . . . and . . .'

The words began to slur and the burning cigarette fell from his fingers. Simm Barry and another cowboy caught Clay's arms as he slumped.

'Tie him in the saddle and we'll head for home,' Janet said quietly. 'He's earned a rest.'

CHAPTER 12

FAST RIDE TO HELL

The cowboy called Brandy waited a mite nervously on the porch of the big Circle R ranch house. He leaned against an awning post, turning his battered hat in his hands.

Then he heard footsteps approaching the front door and he straightened, licked his lips as Kit Ryker stepped out onto the porch, holding his table napkin in one hand.

'You know better'n to interrupt my meals, Brandy, so I figure it must be damned important. Am I right?'

'Yessir, Mr Ryker.'

'Well, don't keep this earth-shaking news to yourself, man! What's up?'

'Longo, Mr Ryker. He's dead.'

Ryker stiffened and he sniffed loudly through his crooked nose. Ever since Jared Clay had butted him in the face, he had had trouble with his sinuses. Doc Bateson said he had a permanently deviated septum and unless he wanted to journey to one of the big Eastern hospitals and was prepared to suffer intense pain, and have several yards of lint rammed up his nose after the surgeon chiselled away the damaged cartilage, it would stay that way, leaking without warning, blocking off at the other extreme.

It was *damned* embarrassing! Why, at his sister's wedding in San Antone, he was mingling with the important guests (in fact, actually speaking with the Congressman who had become his sister's father-in-law) when suddenly his nose had started dripping, *gushing* might be a better word! If there had been a crack handy in the polished oak floor of the reception hall he would have gladly slid down it! *He reiterated a promise he had made himself after he had seen his bruised and battered face for the first time: he would kill Jared Clay if it took him the rest of his life!*

Right now, he used the table napkin to wipe his nostrils, glaring.

'What the hell happened? And don't beat all around the bush! Tell me straight!'

'Somethin' went wrong with that brushfire he was s'posed to start on the girl's place.'

'*What* went wrong, damn you?'

Brandy swallowed. 'Someone showed up and him an' Longo traded lead, the cows stampeded, run right over Longo. Wasn't much left of him by the time I rode down from the drift fence where he'd told me to keep watch.'

131

'Sounds to me you didn't do much of a job of it!'

'The Horton gal and some of her men showed up but that feller, Clay, was already there. Think it was him shot Longo and stampeded the cows outta the draw before the fire trapped 'em.'

Ryker kicked the nearest rattan chair and it skidded violently into a corner, overturned. '*Goddamn*! Clay! That son of a bitch is on the loose? On my range!'

Not quite yours, yet, Brandy thought, but made sure the words didn't slip out so Ryker could hear.

'Seems he escaped from the chain gang when they was clearin' twister damage in Waco.'

'Christ, I don't care *how* he got loose! Just that the son of a bitch *is* ridin' around!' His nostrils were wet again, bubbling with his heavy breathing as the rage built up in him. Then he made an effort to calm down as he realized Brandy was actually cowering, figuring he would be blamed – and rightly so, too! – but Ryker knew he would gain nothing by raging at this dumb cowpoke.

'Where is he now?'

'The gal sent a couple of men off with what was left of Longo wrapped in a blanket, to the sheriff, I s'pose.'

'Not Longo, you idiot! Where's Clay?'

'Aw, Simm Barry and that big feller, Lance someone, got Clay tied into the saddle and the whole shebang rode off towards J Bar H. I stayed hid till they'd rid clear of the ranges before I cut across the Jogtrot an' come right here.'

Ryaker's eyes narrowed. 'Took you one helluva time then!' He gestured curtly to the big barn. 'Sun's already over the roof!'

Brandy fidgetted. 'Well, I . . . I din' want 'em catchin' sight of me. They was riled-up, boss. I figured mebbe enough to send someone after me if I was spotted.'

'So you took your damn time!' Ryker made a lunging step forward and his big fist slammed into Brandy's jaw and knocked him down the short set of steps. As the man sprawled in the dust, sat up, blinking and dazed, the rancher turned his angry face towards the dogrun where some of the nighthawks who had been relieved were now just starting breakfast, watching the drama on the porch with undisguised curiosity.

'Leave that grub *right now*! We're ridin'.'

'Judas, boss, we been ridin' herd all night!' one man was stupid enough to say, a whining complaint clear in his words and manner.

'And it's the last thing you do on Circle R, Calloway, except to pack your bedroll and get off my land! You got ten minutes.'

The man was dumbfounded, but said nothing more: although his face was a dark red with anger, he knew better than to let loose when Ryker was in this kind of mood.

He slammed down his fork, gulped the last mouthful of coffee and stormed back into the bunkhouse, muttering angrily.

'You four get your guns. Brandy, go find Sundeen and bring him back in from wherever he's workin'. You come too. You've done nothin' to earn your breakfast or anythin' else.'

Ryker stomped back into the house and Brandy

released a long breath, blowing out his unshaven cheeks, wincing and rubbing his sore, swelling jaw. He glanced at the four weary nighthawks, shrugged, then strode back to where he had left his mount with trailing reins.

He hoped to hell he could find Sundeen quickly: the way Ryker was right now, the man could start shooting his own men without turning a hair.

And thank God his name wasn't Jared Clay!

'We know he's here, woman! Now go bring him out before I give my men orders to climb down and drag him out!'

Clay stirred, half-stupid with the deep sleep he had fallen into . . . and *hell!* He was in a bed! He shook his head in the semi-darkness of the stuffy, closed bunkhouse, seeing personal gear lying about the other bunks and on the floor, newspaper pictures stuck to the clapboard walls, smelled neatsfoot oil, old tobacco smoke and stale sweat, all familiar odours of a ranch crew living in a confined space.

Then he heard a woman's voice, obviously answering the man who had spoken previously.

'Whether Clay is here or not has nothing to do with you, Ryker. Now take your men and get off my land.'

Ryker! And that was Janet Horton's voice.

It came back with a rush then, the fire at the draw, Longo, the arrival of Janet and her men, and he had passed out with fatigue, vaguely recalling how she had invited him to rest up at J Bar H.

Now Ryker was laughing, but there was little mirth in

the sound.

'Lady, you're outnumbered! Call in every miserable cowhand you've got and I'll still top you two to one! All right, Sundeen, take a couple men and check out that bunkhouse. If you don't find Clay, start on the main house. These yokels won't give you no trouble!'

'Maybe you got that wrong, Ryker!'

'Lance! Don't be foolish. I appreciate your loyalty but you know you won't stand a chance against Sundeen.'

'We just can't stand still and let him—' Lance started to protest and then the words cut off abruptly and Janet frowned as she saw him staring past her shoulder, his mouth open.

She turned quickly and sucked down a sharp, involuntary breath.

Hatless, Clay was standing in the doorway of the bunkhouse, holding a well-used double-barrelled Ithaca shotgun she recognized as belonging to her wrangler, Buck Tompkins, and which he usually kept on wall pegs above his bunk.

Clay looked dishevelled and not very dangerous as he jerked the shotgun to draw attention to it: *unless you looked into his eyes*, then he looked very dangerous indeed. He addressed the mounted Ryker and his eight men. Sundeen was half-dismounted and slowly lowered his boot all the way to the ground, standing beside his horse.

'Shoulda stretched your neck long ago, Clay.'

'I've still got your reminder, Sundeen.' Clay tilted his head a little, exposing the ropeburn on his neck above

135

the dirty, frayed shirt collar. He flicked his gaze to Ryker, his mouth moving into a crooked smile. 'Ain't as handsome as you used to be, Kit.'

Ryker's ears burned crimson. 'You miserable son of a bitch! You ain't gonna walk away from this on your own two feet!'

'I'll have company.' Clay gestured with the shotgun.

'How we know it's even loaded?'

Clay's smile widened. 'Reach for your gun and find out.'

Ryker looked as if he would explode. Even Sundeen ran a tongue around his lips, right hand twitching slightly, but staying well clear of his Colt's butt. The other men sat their horses uncomfortably.

They knew the spread of buckshot fired at that range would knock several of them out of their saddles.

Janet watched silently, hands clenched down at her side in tension. Her men had their own guns out now and it didn't set easy with Ryker's men to be covered by the J Bar H crew who they had always looked down on.

Ryker wrenched off his neckerchief and suddenly clapped it to the lower half of his face.

'Got a little cold, Kit?' she asked tauntingly.

Ryker's eyes actually seemed to burn above the cloth as he angrily wiped his moist nostrils.

'You're finished here!' he said, voice muffled by the neckerchief covering his mouth. 'Get used to the idea, you bitch! Don't matter what happens here today, *you're all through*! You got my word on that!'

She looked disconcerted but Clay said, 'Your word's not worth a pinch of pig's dung, Ryker. Never was.'

Sundeen growled and made an involuntary half-step forward but stopped when Clay flicked his gaze to him.

'Let him fight his own battles, Sundeen. 'Bout time he did.'

'I'll fight you any time you say, jailbird!'

'Sure, I know that. Be glad to accommodate you some other time. Right now, I got things to square with Ryker.'

'You got things to square with *me*?' Ryker wrenched the sodden cloth away from his face, savagely angry. 'Get rid of the damn shotgun and we'll soon see who squares what!'

Clay smiled thinly and walked across to where Janet and her cowboys stood, keeping the Circle R men covered all the time.

'You know how to use one of these, I guess.'

'Don't be foolish, Clay!' she said as he offered her the Ithaca. 'His men outnumber us and none of them can be trusted!'

Clay looked past her to the man called Lance. 'You want to hold the shotgun on 'em?'

'Damn' right!' Lance, a big, middle-aged cowpoke with a tough face that reflected the hard knocks he had survived over the years, took the gun and, as Sundeen stirred, swung the barrels onto the big man. 'Shuck the gunbelt, Sundeen. Rest of you do the same!'

There were murmurings and curses but when they realized they were under the drawn weapons of the rest of the J Bar H crew, Ryker's men complied. They dumped their gunbelts and, at further orders from Lance, unsheathed their rifles carefully and dropped

137

them to the ground, also.

'Now fold your hands on your saddlehorns and keep 'em that way,' Lance ordered. 'Just twitch an' you'll eat buckshot.' He nodded to Clay. 'Ryker's all yours, Clay. If he ain't too yaller to climb on down.'

'You better not ride the range alone from now on, mister!' Ryker gritted.

Lance merely smiled and then Ryker jammed his spurs into his paint and the mount lunged forward with a startled whinny. Clay threw himself aside but the horse's shoulder hit him and knocked him against the front of the bunkhouse.

He rolled away as Janet screamed a warning and Ryker drew his Colt. Ryker had not shucked his gunbelt with his crew: Lance had been concentrated on the men, figuring Clay would watch Ryker.

Clay hurled himself around the corner of the bunkhouse as Ryker fired and the bullet chewed splinters from a plank. The horse was still lunging and swerved wildly. Ryker, caught unawares, rocked in the saddle, grabbed instinctively at the saddlehorn to keep from falling.

Clay lunged and grabbed the man's leg, heaved mightily: the rancher yelled as he was thrown from the saddle. Clay slapped the stumbling paint on the rump. It lunged away and he stepped in, kicked the gun from Ryker's hand, then kicked the man in the chest, the impact sending the rancher rolling violently.

He groped for the six-gun and Clay stomped on his hand, kicked the Colt away, grabbed Ryker's hair as his hat fell off. The rancher was thinning on top and Clay's hand came away with a bunch of stringy strands between his fingers, Ryker's cry of pain ringing in his ears.

But that pain stung the rancher to effort and he made a brief whining sound as he lashed out blindly. His fist took Clay on an ear and he stumbled, head ringing, his ear feeling as if someone had hit him with the side of a plank.

Just as Ryker's pain had sent his adrenalin racing wildly through his veins, Clay's agony set his already hard-pumping heart to further effort and he met the rancher as Ryker took a long stride towards him.

Clay ducked under a whistling right, weaved away from a following left, and, head down, worked his arms like they were steam-driven, beating a savage tattoo on Ryker's thickening midriff, working up across the chest, belting blow after blow into the man's lower ribcage. As Ryker faltered, his legs wobbling, he started to bend in the middle.

Clay rammed a hard shoulder under his jaw, heard the man's teeth click together as Ryker's head snapped back. The big rancher staggered but he was game, and even as he fought to keep his balance, he swung a wild arm and the fist caught Clay as he closed, bouncing off his jaw, not hurting a lot, but spoiling the smoothness of his move. He stumbled, and Ryker regained his balance swiftly, teeth bared, and took a long, lunging step back, fists cocked, then blurring in a punishing barrage that sent Clay staggering, finally forcing him down to one knee.

Ryker swung a long leg at his head.

Clay saw it coming, hunched his left shoulder, felt the jarring impact, his arm numbing to the wrist. He spun to one side and Ryker missed with his follow-through kick. He fell against the bunkhouse, and when he tried to turn, found himself pinned there by Clay's weight.

Clay used his left side to hamper the rancher, giving his arm time to recover some circulation, lifted his right arm and chopped it across the back of Ryker's head. That poor, battered face wasn't improved any by its collision with the weathered, iron-hard planks.

It was blood that poured from his nostrils now as he slithered along the bunkhouse wall, legs starting to fold. Clay lifted a knee into his belly, used it to pin the man in his half-fallen position, clubbed him several times in the face. The rancher's head jerked limply on his neck. Clay fisted up the front of the sweaty, blood-spattered shirt and flung the Circle R owner out into the yard. Ryker hit hard, rolled once, then flopped back, face down in the dust.

There was silence from the group. Sundeen frowned deeply and lifted his bleak gaze to Clay.

He started forward to help Ryker but Clay put up a hand. 'Stay right there.'

'Goddamn you, Clay! Lemme help him!'

'Leave him be. How about you and me now, Sundeen?'

The girl gasped and most of the men, from both ranches, exchanged shocked glances. Sundeen stared and then a slow smile curled his lips.

'Clay!' Janet said sharply. 'Don't be foolish!'

He ignored her, his blood up and racing as he stared stubbornly, wickedly at Sundeen. 'You game?'

Sundeen laughed, lifted his big fists. 'Try me!'

'Pick up your gunbelt.'

Clay's cold words stopped the big Circle R man in his tracks. 'W-what?'

'I'm feelin' a mite . . . tuckered,' Clay panted, 'for another fist fight right now. So grab your gunbelt and we'll finish it once and for all.'

'Clay, for God's sake!' Janet started forward but stopped abruptly when she saw his face. *Reckless. Eager!*

He was past caring about risk: after all this time, he was taking the revenge he had dreamed about on the chain gang, and he aimed to make the most of it.

And she knew there was nothing she could do about it. Still, she tried.

'Clay, you can't! Please! Don't do this!'

'Well, Sundeen, what'll it be? Bullets and a fast ride to hell, or back down and show that yellow streak you got all the way down your back to your ass?'

Sundeen was furious, muttered savage curses as he stormed across to where he had dropped his gun rig and scooped it up.

There wasn't a sound in the yard: it seemed everyone was holding their breath.

Then Lance spoke quietly, his words clear and distinct as they dropped into the silence.

'We got company.'

Clay, tensed, ready for the gunfight, stiffened and looked in the direction Lance pointed with the shotgun.

141

A group of riders was coming into the main yard of the ranch, under a sun-tinted pall of dust.

Sunlight flashed from something metallic, it might have been a gun barrel.

Or a sheriff's badge.

Two words seared through Jared Clay's seething brain.

'*Goddamn posse*!'

CHAPTER 13

JAGO

There were six riders, two of them wearing law badges.

Clay and everyone else recognized the butterball shape of Owen Jago right away. But not all of them knew the man riding alongside him was Sheriff Durango Spence.

They hauled rein, none of the group of men in the ranch yard having moved more than a few inches since Lance had pointed out the arrival of the posse.

Owen Jago thumbed back his broad-brimmed black hat and the sun washed over his moon face with its bristling sideburns and muttonchops, the whiskers a darker shade than the pepper-and-salt hair showing beneath the tilted hat. There was sweat on his face and dark patches in his armpits, marking his ivory-coloured shirt.

He idly scratched at an itchy spot just within his

hairline as he raked brown, button eyes around the riders, and the bloody form of Ryker being helped to his feet by Sundeen.

'Tea party, folks?' He spoke in the light, precise voice that Clay remembered from the trial, his red lips moist and rubbery looking. Clay recalled them, too, and how they had moved over the legal words without hesitation, but never twitched in even a small smile.

'Uninvited guests, sheriff,' Janet said quickly, looking hard at Ryker who was mopping his blood-streaked face with a kerchief Sundeen handed him. 'Intimidation and an attempt at arson. So, your arrival is timely, Sheriff.'

Jago frowned slightly, the creases briefly marking his otherwise smooth forehead.

'Explain, please, Miss Horton.'

'I'll explain, Owen!' snapped Ryker, his words slurred because of swollen lips and tongue. 'We—'

Jago held up one pudgy hand and the button eyes lifted to Ryker's face. 'In good time, Kit. Don't you know it's "ladies first"?'

Ryker's mouth tightened despite the swelling and bruising as Jago turned his attention to the girl, motioning for her to speak.

'You know about Longo by now, how he came by his injuries. He was trying to set fire to a brush fence across a draw where I was holding cattle for branding.'

'My mavericks! That's what she was holdin'!' cut in Ryker. 'Everyone rounds-up mavericks in those ranges and they know damn well they're Circle R stock gone wild! I'm sick of supplyin' the whole blamed county

144

with beef, either for the table or the market.'

Jago didn't even look at the rancher, kept his gaze on Janet. 'And you decided to deal with it in your own way. All right, Kit, we'll discuss it in detail later. Meantime. . .' He gestured for Janet to continue.

She told her story briefly and accurately.

For the first time Jago looked at Clay.

'You're the fugitive from the Brazosville chain gang. I recollect you at your trial.'

Clay stretched his neck so the ropeburn showed. 'Just to jog your memory, sheriff.'

'Yes. An attempt at vigilante-style lynching, but Mr Ryker showed sense enough to stop it and bring you to court. What were you doing in the hills where Longo allegedly set this fire?'

'Not "allegedly" – he did it. I was only skirting the foothills when I saw him lighting a bundle of sticks and tossing it into the brush fence. I rode up there to see what was going on and we got into our hassle.'

'Which terminated in Longo's death.'

'The herd stampeded. He wasn't quick enough to get out of the way.'

'But you were. Was it the fire that started the stampede?'

Clay almost smiled at Jago's question. 'Well, the fire had took hold and the only way out was through the brush fence. I roped it and pulled it aside and triggered a couple of shots. Fire or bullets set the herd off, take your pick. I wouldn't like to say which.'

Jago pursed his womanish lips and Spence leaned from his saddle, said something in a low voice.

145

Jago looked first at Janet and then back to Clay.

'My colleague here has just reminded me that it's unlikely you had anything to do with the fire, except to try to prevent Longo from succeeding at his arson attempt. Sheriff Spence pointed out that you would hardly have signed over the reward money on Hal Getty to Miss Horton if you had notions of destroying her stock. And I have to admit it's highly unlikely you would have allied yourself with one of Circle R's men.'

The girl was staring blankly at Clay, then blinked and said, 'What's this? I know nothing about any reward money.'

Durango Spence cleared his throat and told about Getty being wanted for the murder of Sheriff Lonnie Cousins.

'I'm satisfied Clay could've killed Getty but didn't, and the man confessed to his crimes. He was in such pain, believed he was dying. I told Clay he would be eligible for the bounty. He said to give you the reward money, ma'am, as he owed you a favour. He put it all in writing before he left us.'

Her breasts rose and tightened the material of her shirt as she filled her lungs with a deep breath. 'I . . . I don't understand.' She frowned slightly at Clay. 'You . . . you don't owe me anything.'

'You helped me when I needed it.'

She whipped her head around towards Jago.

'It's all legitimate, Janet. Sitting in the bank safe right now, ready to deposit in your ranch account.'

She stared a moment longer, then smiled, her entire face lighting up. 'I still can't believe it! But it's come at

146

the best possible time.' She sobered some as she glanced at Ryker and Sundeen. 'All the damage done to my fences and my loss of stock because they were able to get out and eat poison weed, or bog down in the quagmires after the rains. I can get J Bar H back on its feet now! Thanks to your generosity!' She gave Clay a dazzling smile. 'I believe I could kiss you, Jared Clay!'

He smiled faintly, held up a hand. 'Thanks is just fine, ma'am . . . for the moment.'

'We'll talk later.' She turned to Jago. 'Well, what're you going to do about all this, Owen? You've seen Longo and you've heard Clay's version of what happened. Where do we go from here?'

Jago held her gaze a long moment, flicked his eyes towards Kit Ryker. 'I expect you'll deny all knowldge of this, Kit?'

'Damn right! I sent Longo into the hills to do a rough count of mavericks. They seem to be scattered all over the county since the rains and that twister messin' up the weather. You ask me, this damn rustler was workin' for the gal, roundin' up my mavericks, holdin' 'em in that draw, an' Longo come across him. No love lost between them two, so I reckon there was a fight and somehow the fire started – and this Clay figured his story afterward. He reckoned the gal'd back him up, naturally, and looks like he was right.'

Jago nodded slowly, holding up a hand as Janet started to protest angrily. 'I detect a touch of . . . desperation . . . in your attempt to show Miss Horton in as bad a light as possible, Kit.'

Ryker rubbed hard at his forehead. 'Hell. What do

you expect? Look at me! Clay did this, beat the hell outta me while her men held a shotgun on my crew! Whatever's goin' on, they're in it together. You showin' up now is just bad timin' far as I'm concerned. Couldn't be better for them.'

'By the way, Kit, we were originally on our way to Circle R to inform you about Longo's misfortune and hear your side of the story.' Jago spoke quietly, studying the rancher's face. Ryker said nothing, waiting, breathing shallow, sensing something coming that he wasn't going to like.

And he was right: he didn't like it at all.

'Ran into Ben Calloway on the way, Kit. He was mighty put out. Says you fired him in a fit of temper, then refused to pay him what was owed him for ranch work.'

'Son of a bitch was a lousy cowhand, lousy an' lazy. S'posed to be on nighthawk, slept in his saddle most times. I just had me a bellyful.'

'This the same Ben Calloway you were talking about making *segundo* of Circle R so you could take some time off to visit your sister in San Antone, Kit?'

Ryker's face was a study, a series of quick expressions, none of which was easy to read, what with the bruising and swelling and cuts. But the man was badly shaken, that was clear enough.

So he blustered instead of trying to ride out Jago's words.

'Glad you reminded me about Carrie, Owen. I dunno what kinda kinfolk to me you'd call her new father-in-law, but whatever it is, he's still a

Congressman.' He let the words hang and smiled crookedly. 'Him an' me seem to hit it off well enough so far. Told me, any problems I had, to contact him and. . . .' His smiled widened as he shrugged. 'Just might have to take him up on the offer.'

Jago, his moon face looking a lot harder than most folk would expect, held up his hand again.

'I believe I take your meaning, Kit.'

'Thought you might.' Ryker was smirking confidently now as he looked towards Janet.

'Oh, I'm sure I do,' Jago went on, his hardening tone bringing Ryker's head around with a snap. 'And I thought you knew me well enough to realize that such veiled threats to me are like water off a duck's back. *Except*, in my experience, such pressure almost always comes from a man with something to hide.'

Ryker set his aching jaw and glared. 'I'd go easy, I was you, Owen.'

'I never "go easy", Kit. I work my butt off to prove a man guilty or innocent, and I like to think I am entirely without prejudice.'

'You have that reputation!' Clay allowed with a trace of bitterness. 'But you messed up with me. You believed that "rustling" charge and I was framed.'

Jago's expression didn't change. 'Clay, I learned you'd had some trouble with using a wideloop some years ago in Arizona. Perhaps I let that influence me when I shouldn't have.'

Clay frowned. 'Hell, I was only a kid! My pa was keeping poorly and some range bully took a bunch of our cows while I was away. By the time I went after 'em, that damn smug bastard's brother had been elected sheriff! I didn't stand a chance.'

Jago looked very sober now. 'Perhaps I was influenced more than I should've been, but I was satisfied with the evidence presented. Since then, I have had good reports about your prison term and your work during the Waco twister clean-up, especially the rescue of the Harding family when their house was half buried in a mud-slide.' He paused and let his words sink in. 'But, I have to remind you, you absconded from a prison work party and are still technically a fugitive.'

'Oh, for heaven's sake, Owen!' snapped Janet. 'Everyone knows Ryker framed Clay on that rustling charge!'

'I found sufficient evidence—'

'To satisfy you! Yes, yes, I know how you work, Owen. Stubborn as a Nevada mule, live by The Law Book, at the same time ignoring another book, a bigger, wiser one that stresses honour and compassion as much as punishment and retaliation.'

Jago drew himself up – the effect was of a balloon growing in size as more air was pumped in. 'I pride myself on my fairness, Janet! I like to think I am a man of honour.'

'Yes, I think that's true. But you would be a better man if you leaned a little more towards leniency and took into account mitigating circumstances.'

'I do not require you to tell me my job, Janet Horton. I know—'

'For Chris'sakes, what the hell're you doin'?' demanded Ryker. 'Jesus, I want this settled right now!

150

This woman's accusin' me of trying to run her off her ranch and I deny it. And I'll continue to deny it.' His eyes pinched down and his voice hardened as he raked his gaze over Jago's flushed face. 'You push this, Owen, and I'll guarantee you'll be out of a job in just the time it takes me to send a wire to Congressman Ball in Washington.'

Jago sighed, stiffened as he shook his head slowly. 'You're a bigger blamed fool than I thought, Kit. I warned you about such threats. After we spoke with Ben Calloway – he has no liking or loyalty to you, by now, of course – he agreed to make a statement about all the times you paid him, and others, extra money to cut J Bar H fences, burn their pastures, run off their stock, have their crew beaten in supposedly drunken brawls in town, and warned not to go back to work for J Bar H. I sent a man back to town with Ben and he'll be in Lawyer Bascom's office right now, I should think, making his testimonial, all legal and admissable in a court of law.'

The sheriff glanced from the bloodless face of Ryker to Janet and for once his rubbery lips moved in the suggestion of a smile.

'Calloway is making this statement in exchange for immunity from prosecution. Perhaps I recall reading that other "Book" you mentioned, Janet. I thank you for reminding me about it, just the same.'

She smiled, glanced at Jared Clay, but his face was unreadable.

Sundeen's wasn't.

It was clouded with anger and, probably, the

151

knowledge that it was going to be a mighty hard chore to walk away from this looming trouble.

He glanced towards Ryker. 'Say the word, boss,' he murmured in a low voice.

Ryker hesitated, not quite ready to have everything blow up in his face – *but*. Holding the threat of Carrie's father-in-law over Jago's head had been a mistake, a bad mistake, he realized now. It had only served to get Jago's dander up, a new experience for all who witnessed it, for the sheriff's integrity and unshakable composure were legendary throughout Brazos County.

It didn't bear contemplating what he might do now he had finally been driven to giving his emotions free rein.

Ryker swayed, and grabbed suddenly at the startled Sundeen's arm. The rancher swayed and rolled his eyes.

'Whoa! Hell, I feel mighty . . . woozy.' He glared at Clay. 'Thanks to you no doubt. Ahh!' He swayed again, still holding to Sundeen's upper arm. 'Janet, could I trouble you for a little brandy or whiskey? Just a slug to kind of settle me.'

He let his legs buckle and Sundeen steadied him, making himself look concerned now. 'Hey! Easy, boss. That damn Clay must've done you more damage than you figured.'

Janet frowned slightly but nodded, having witnessed the bad beating Ryker had taken at the hands of Jared Clay. 'I'll fetch something.'

She crossed the porch and went into the house and Ryker straightened, wiping a hand across his eyes. 'I . . . I'll be OK. Sundeen, you better bring that whiskey pronto, OK?' Ryker stood alone now, but still swaying and looking on the verge of collapse, as he drew out his last word, looking hard at his ramrod. Then Sundeen's puzzled look disappeared. He even smiled crookedly as he hurried up onto the porch and went into the house after the girl.

Clay suddenly started after him but Jago moved with suprising speed for a man his shape and size and his hand lifted a cocked six-gun, menacing the fugitive.

'You stay put, Clay!'

'Damnit, Jago, Sundeen's the one you ought to stop!'

Jago hesitated, glanced towards Ryker, who seemed to be standing firmly enough for the moment. Jago frowned, and then there were the sounds of a scuffle, a muffled cry, and Sundeen appeared on the porch, the struggling girl held in front of him with his left arm, his Colt pressed into her side.

'Time we were leavin', I reckon, boss.'

'Reckon so.' Ryker moved and scooped up his pistol from the ground as Jago swung the Colt in his direction.

'No you don't!'

Ryker had nothing to lose now. Still crouching, moving perhaps a little stiffly because of the beating he had taken, he fired, the gun bucking against his hand.

At that range it was impossible to miss a man Jago's size. The sheriff grunted, spun in his saddle, dropping his Colt as he grabbed for the saddlehorn, but missed. He rolled against Spence sitting astride his mount alongside. Durango was drawing his own gun and as Jago's bulk brushed him, he fumbled, had to use both

153

hands on the reins as his horse jumped and whinnied.

Owen Jago spilled to the ground with a solid thud.

Lance swung the shotgun but didn't know where to point it, only too aware that Janet was in extreme danger. For the same reason, seeing Sundeen wrenching the girl with him as he turned slightly, Clay didn't make a move for his own gun.

He lifted his hands slightly out from his sides as Spence and the posse men and the ranch hands all looked on, stymied, afraid for the girl.

Ryker had made the only move that would get him out of the predicament he had gotten himself into, though his shooting Jago landed him in an even deeper mire. Still walking stiffly, he went to his horse and mounted with a grunt, settling into leather and sliding his rifle from the scabbard, preferring its greater load, eleven cartridges against six in his Colt, four now he had shot Jago.

He levered in a shell and watched Sundeen effortlessly lift the girl onto his horse, then swing up lithely behind her. Spence had dismounted and was kneeling beside Jago who was writhing on the ground, leaving large splotches of blood in the dirt.

'Anyone tries to follow ... well, you know what'll happen to the gal,' Ryker smiled crookedly, swinging the rifle towards Clay.

'What about us, boss?' called one of the Circle R crew. 'You can't leave us!'

'Leave any time you like, just don't follow Sundeen and me.'

There was a milling of horses and men as the Circle

R crew prepared to move out, swearing, realizing they were being abandoned, had to make their own moves from here on in. The grunting and rough manoeuvring of the horses made the mounts of the posse restless. Dust rose.

Ryker cursed and used his knees to move his mount so he would have a clear shot at Clay, but . . . *where the hell had Jared Clay got to?*

'Where is he?' Ryker called to Sundeen who had his hands full with Janet as she suddenly began to struggle, making things as hard as she could for her captor.

'*There!*' Sundeen yelled. 'By the porch!'

Ryker whirled and Clay rose from beside the low steps, Colt blasting as the rancher triggered a wild shot. It scattered the posse men as the bullet ploughed up a line of flying splinters from the porch floor. Clay used the cover of the milling men to roll out into the open, come up onto one knee, arm lifting.

Over the foresight of the Colt he saw Kit Ryker's battered face blanch and then it was hidden by the cloud of flame-torn gunsmoke. Ryker crashed to the ground, flailing, and Sundeen, fighting the prancing mount, cuffing Janet in his anger, tried to bring his Colt over to get a shot at Clay. Dazed, Janet pressed back, unsettling Sundeen's steadiness.

He jabbed her hard in the ribs, confident Clay would not take a shot at him as long as the girl straddled the mount in front of his big body, one thick arm crushing her against him.

But Clay was already moving.

Sundeen was right: he couldn't risk a shot while the

girl was still held in the saddle. But he jumped up onto the porch where a couple of men lay prone, hoping no stray bullets found them, used one hand on the rail to aid his lift as he swung his legs and body up and over in a flying leap.

Janet's eyes widened and she may have screamed, but Sundeen's face registered only shock and disbelief as Clay's body hurtled towards him. He twisted frantically, bringing up his Colt. The girl ducked, and toppled off the prancing mount, flinging herself to the side.

Clay floundered as he hit the ground. His boots had slammed into Sundeen, the weight of his entire moving body behind them. Sundeen hit the ground solidly but thrust up, the girl moving very slowly, dazed, hampering him. The big Circle R man reached out for her with one hand, swung his gun towards Clay, who was down on the ground, too, rolling onto his belly.

Clay's Colt roared twice in quick succession and Sundeen, despite his huge bulk, was hurled backwards, chest bloody. But the big man grunted, heaved over to the left and dragged the barrel of his Colt through the dirt as he tried to bring it to bear on the girl: she was closest and easiest to kill.

Clay's next shot took Sundeen through the head, and he was smashed over backwards, gun flying from dead fingers, Janet cringing away from splashing blood and bits of flying bone.

She was bruised and still a mite dazed from the violence of her fall, one arm bleeding from a gravel cut, a small scrape on her left cheekbone. Clay steadied her as he pulled her to her feet.

'Sorry. I had to move fast.'

She gave him a shaky smile. 'Thank God you did.'

He eased her down onto the porch steps and went to where Spence was bending over Jago, pressing rags torn from the fat man's own shirt to the wound in his chest.

'How is he?'

Spence glanced up. 'He'll be all right, I think.' He smiled crookedly. 'All that fat probably kept the bullet from going too deep.' He touched the pale Jago's shoulder to let him know he was only joshing, turned back to Clay. 'I've sent a man into the house to look for a medical kit.'

Lance overheard and said he knew where it was and hurried inside. Clay looked down at Jago, who was watching him with his pain-filled eyes.

'A rougher justice than I'm used to,' Jago gasped. Then he tried to smile, just a slight movement of his rubbery lips and not entirely successful. 'But adequate under the cir-circumstances. I'm satisfied. Thank you, Clay.'

Jared Clay nodded and steadied Janet as she came up alongside.

'There's a lot to sort out, Owen.'

Jago nodded. 'It'll take time, but it will be in the end. I . . . I don't know if I can be entirely happy knowing a fugitive named Jared Clay is still in my County.'

Clay stiffened and he felt the girl squeeze his arm, sharing his tension. She looked at Spence who shrugged and turned to Jago.

'I think we have a good man here, Owen, whether he's Jared Clay or not.'

Jago frowned and so did Clay. The girl was the first to get it and smiled at Jago.

'How about . . . Josh Cutler?'

Clay looked at her sharply. 'Wh-at?'

Jago's puzzlement momentarily washed the lines of pain from his sweating moon face. 'Who – who's "Josh Cutler"?'

The girl's smile widened. 'Why my new partner, of course. He's already invested money in J Bar H.'

She indicated Clay, who finally understood.

He put out a hand towards towards the wounded lawman. ' "Jake" Cutler, actually, sheriff.' Smiling at the girl, he said, quietly, 'Can't see myself as a "Josh".'

'Whatever you say. Is that all right, Sheriff? Jake Cutler – no Jared Clay in your county then.'

Jago slowly lifted a big hand and weakly touched Clay's – *Cutler's* – proffered one.

Spence said with a crooked smile, 'Nothing like a bullet in the brisket to make a man see reason.'

'I believe I can live with this new . . . arrangement,' Jago gasped, very tired now. He closed his eyes slowly.

As Janet tightened her grip on his arm, the no-longer fugitive, Mr Cutler, said,

'Me, too.'